LOYAL CREATURES

Morris Gleitzman

PUFFIN

PUFFIN BOOKS

Published by the Penguin Group
Penguin Books Ltd, 80 Strand, London WC2R 0RL, England
Penguin Group (USA) Inc., 375 Hudson Street, New York, New York 10014, USA
Penguin Group (Canada), 90 Eglinton Avenue East, Suite 700, Toronto, Ontario, Canada M4P 2Y3
(a division of Pearson Penguin Canada Inc.)
Penguin Ireland, 25 St Stephen's Green, Dublin 2, Ireland (a division of Penguin Books Ltd)
Penguin Group (Australia), 707 Collins Street, Melbourne, Victoria 3008, Australia
(a division of Pearson Australia Group Pty Ltd)
Penguin Books India Pvt Ltd, 11 Community Centre, Panchsheel Park, New Delhi – 110 017, India
Penguin Group (NZ), 67 Apollo Drive, Rosedale, Auckland 0632, New Zealand
(a division of Pearson New Zealand Ltd)
Penguin Books (South Africa) (Pty) Ltd, Block D, Rosebank Office Park, 181 Jan Smuts Avenue,
Parktown North, Gauteng 2193, South Africa

Penguin Books Ltd, Registered Offices: 80 Strand, London WC2R 0RL, England

puffinbooks.com

First published in Australia by Penguin Group (Australia) 2014
Published in Great Britain by Puffin Books 2014
001

Text copyright © Morris Gleitzman, 2014
Text design by Tony Palmer © Penguin Group (Australia), 2014
Map on page vi: Map 14, page 360 of volume VII of the *Official History
of Australia in the War of 1914–1919* courtesy of AWM
All rights reserved

The moral right of the author has been asserted

Typeset in 13/16.5pt Minion Regular
Printed in Great Britain by Clays Ltd, St Ives plc

British Library Cataloguing in Publication Data
A CIP catalogue record for this book is available from the British Library

ISBN: 978-0-141-35500-9

www.greenpenguin.co.uk

MIX
Paper from
responsible sources
FSC
www.fsc.org   FSC® C018179

Penguin Books is committed to a sustainable
future for our business, our readers and our
planet. This book is made from paper certified
by the Forest Stewardship Council.

For Michael and Clare Morpurgo

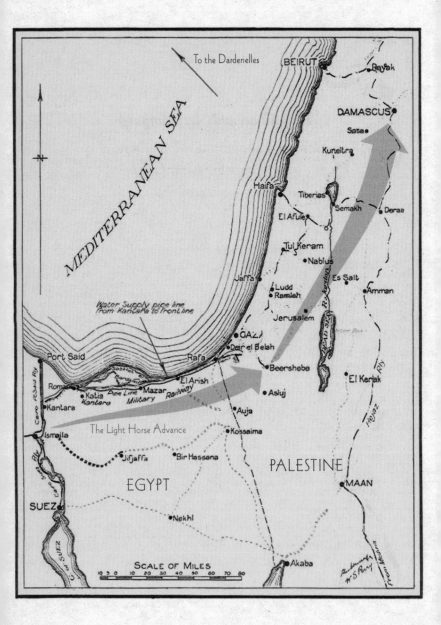

*They suffered wounds, thirst,
hunger and weariness almost beyond
endurance but never failed.
They did not come home.*

Inscription on a memorial in
Sydney's Royal Botanic Gardens
to the Australian horses in World War One

1

Nineteen fourteen.

War.

Did I want to go?

Course I did.

Who wouldn't want to choof off to distant exotic places, give a pack of mongrel bullies what for and have the sort of experiences you just didn't get in the Cudgegong district.

When I told Dad I wanted to go, he tried to wallop me round the head with a canvas bucket.

Not too hard, I was bigger than him. But I was still surprised. Hitting people with buckets wasn't Dad's style. Plus, since Mum died, me and Dad were a team. Mates. You didn't go round whacking your mates in the head with work utensils.

Something was going on.

Dad glared at me.

'You and me'll be first in the trenches,' he said, 'if Germany invades New South Wales. Till then we'll stay out of other dopey idiots' wars.'

I squinted up at the blokes riding past. They didn't look that dopey to me.

Me and Dad were on Mindalee Station, rigging up some irrigation for their kitchen garden. Bunch of the station hands were heading off to Sydney with their horses to volunteer for the fighting.

My horse Daisy looked up from the carrot patch she was chewing on and gave a few snorts. Wishing the other horses luck, probably.

Dad gave the blokes a nod. He knew some of them from the pub.

They nodded back.

'Don't fall down a well, Ted,' said one. 'When we need reinforcements, we'll be giving you a hoi.'

Before Dad could reply, I spoke up.

'No need,' I said. 'We'll probably beat you lazy blighters there.'

The bloke grinned as he rode off.

I braced myself for another gobful of wet canvas, in case Dad was getting a taste for this method of arguing. But he just glared at me again.

'Forget it,' he said. 'You're fifteen.'

Technically he was right. But I knew several blokes who'd volunteered at fifteen. All right, sixteen.

And the tall ones like me had been accepted if they were good at lying about their age.

'I'm sixteen in five months,' I reminded Dad.

He frowned and looked like he was going to whack me again.

Before he could, Mr Conroy the station owner came over.

'Having a smoko, Ballantyne?' said Mr Conroy to Dad. 'It's not Christmas yet.'

Pushy blighter, he could see we weren't. I didn't even smoke. Mum reckoned tobacco was a waste of a bloke's wages. Being careful with money was always important to Mum right to the end, so I promised her I wouldn't smoke, permanent.

I think Mum made Dad promise something too, at the end. About us not going to the war.

'Be done today, Mr Conroy,' said Dad, whacking a length of irrigation pipe instead of me.

Mr Conroy looked at Daisy, who'd moved on to the peas.

'Pity you didn't finish earlier, Ballantyne,' he said. 'You could have volunteered with my blokes. Help sort them Huns and Turks out.'

Dad didn't reply at first.

'Tell those nags to pull their heads in, Frankie,' he said to me.

Dad's horse Jimmy had decided Daisy was on

to a good thing in the veggies. I went over to roust them out.

'Got the lad to look after,' I heard Dad say to Mr Conroy.

I didn't hear what Mr Conroy said back, but while I was putting nosebags on Daisy and Jimmy, I heard grunting sounds.

Dad was hacking into the dirt with the big pickaxe, shoulders knotted and teeth clenched with the effort of swinging the thing.

That was my job. We'd agreed I'd do the heavy work. Dad's back wasn't the best. Old bloke's curse, he reckoned. He was probably right, he was nearly thirty-six.

I hurried over to give him a hand. And saw from his face it wasn't just the hefty metal head of the pickaxe he was ramming down into the dirt.

It was something else as well.

Something he was feeling.

That's when I knew he wanted to go to war as much as I did.

The German and Turk armies weren't the only ones getting my blood up.

Joan Prescott in the chemist's was streets ahead of them. Forget the girls on soap packets. Joan was dead-set gorgeous. At school she had more freckles and knee scabs than the rest of us put together. And more skill at gumnut poker and more patience at training beetles.

And more heart.

She came to Mum's funeral off her own bat.

Trouble was, she'd got a scholarship to the grammar school. Her parents wouldn't let her speak to me any more. But I still liked being in the same place as her, so I spent hours in that shop pretending to inspect ointments.

'Frank, what are you doing?'

I nearly dropped the jar. Joan had crept up behind me.

'Shopping,' I said.

She rolled her eyes, which was something else she was good at. She could sink a deep well into your heart just by moving her eyeballs.

'You shouldn't be in here,' she said.

I knew she was just doing her job. Since her dad volunteered for the war, she was assistant manager after school.

'I'm a customer,' I said. Which wasn't what I wanted to say at all. What I wanted to say was, can I give your cheek a bit of a touch, just gently, if that's all right with you.

But I didn't say that. I never had.

Joan glanced anxiously around the shop as usual, checking if we were being watched.

I tried to think what a grammar-school bloke would say right now.

'Australia's a free country,' I said.

'Frank,' said Joan. 'You know what my father reckons about this.'

I sighed.

Not old enough for boys, that's what he reckoned. Which was bull. Joan had always been old enough for boys. Anyway, he didn't mean all boys. Just boys who left school and dug holes for their dads.

Joan gave me a sad look and pushed something into my hand.

Cough lozenges. Three of them. She knew I liked them.

Before I could say thank you, or please run away with me, somebody grabbed the jar of ointment out of my other hand.

'So,' said Mrs Prescott, thin-lipped, giving the label a read. 'For the treatment of fungal infections of the feet, armpits and groin.'

'I sweat a lot,' I mumbled. 'In my line of work.'

'It's true,' said Joan. 'He does.'

Mrs Prescott glared at Joan, then looked at me hard and cold. Mr Prescott must have told her to keep the unfriendliness going while he was away.

'They use this stuff in the trenches,' said Mrs Prescott. 'But of course, your family wouldn't know about trenches, would they?'

I was about to tell her how me and Dad regularly dug irrigation channels and drainage ditches of all kinds, including trenches. Then I realised what she meant and kept my trap shut.

Joan shuffled miserably. I could see she wanted to say something but didn't dare. I did dare, but I kept quiet too. My aim, long term, was to win Joan's mum's admiration and respect. I probably wouldn't do that if I told her to stick her head up her arse.

'One shilling and ninepence,' said Mrs Prescott.

While I fumbled for the money, Joan looked at me sympathetically and Mrs Prescott looked at me like I was something you find wriggling at the bottom of a bore hole.

But I knew all that could change.

If I came back from the war with a chest full of medals all that could change, permanent.

2

Choose the right moment, that was the go.

Tell Dad what had just been announced in the paper. Exciting new war opportunities for blokes like him and me.

Dead-set perfect for us, the Aussie Light Horse.

Trouble was, I didn't do a great job of picking the right moment.

We were on a property out west, locating water for a farmer who needed it urgent. His cattle were like empty saddlebags.

Dad was squinting at the dusty landscape, checking the scrub patterns like we always did when we were deciding where a dam or bore could go.

I should have saved the war talk for later, but suddenly I couldn't keep my trap shut.

'They're putting a new Light Horse regiment together,' I said to Dad. 'Mounted infantry.'

Dad stopped squinting at the scrub and squinted at me.

'Yeah,' he said. 'I heard.'

I didn't know he had. I pushed on.

'Blokes are volunteering with their horses,' I said. 'Half the blokes I play footy with have gone already.'

'Heard that too,' said Dad.

This time he didn't look at me. Just the scrub.

Daisy twitched against my knee. She was excited at the idea of volunteering. Well, I was pretty sure she would be once we'd done it.

Come on, Dad, I said to myself. Your face won't crack if you show some interest.

He didn't.

'Go and have a dig over there,' he said, pointing.

I knew Dad had picked the right spot even before I got the spade into the dirt. Daisy had her nose to the ground and was stamping her feet. She always got restless when water was close. I reckoned it was something to do with the gush of it when her foal was born, and how much she missed her daughter after the little tyke got sold.

Dad came over and had a squiz at the soil and rocks I was turning up with my spade. Signs were good. Plus it was a flat spot. Handy for the drillers when they arrived with the big steam-driven rig.

'Beauty,' said Dad.

He had a gift for finding water, everyone said so. Pity I didn't have a gift for finding the right moment to open my gob.

'Not just Europe now,' I said. 'The war's in North Africa too.'

Dad didn't say anything.

'Egypt,' I said. 'That's where the Light Horse is going.'

Dad flung his handful of dirt and rocks down so hard they bounced. His face had gone so red, for a sec I thought he was having a heart seizure.

'Enough,' he yelled.

Daisy and Jimmy both took a step back.

'Go and tell the farmer it's his lucky day,' said Dad. 'Before it stops being yours and I ship you off to your cousins in Perth.'

I didn't argue. Not with Dad so riled.

I hopped on Daisy and headed off towards the homestead. At times like this you didn't steer Daisy, just pointed her. So when she flattened Dad's billy with her hoof as we passed, it was her making a point, not me.

As we got closer to the house, I saw the farmer. He was aiming a rifle at something on the ground.

First off I thought it was a snake.

Wished I hadn't left my spade with Dad. No need to waste a bullet on a snake. If that farmer had bullets to waste, we should have been charging him full price.

Then I saw it wasn't a snake.

It was a dog. An old fella, by the look. Just sitting on the ground gazing up at the farmer. And the gun.

Farmers. Dogs work round the place for years, loyal as elastic-sided boots. Then when the poor mutts are too old, do they get a spell of thanks and decent meat?

Do they heck.

None of my business, but for the second time that day I couldn't keep my trap shut.

'Hey,' I yelled. 'Don't.'

Me and Daisy rode over fast.

The farmer gave us a hard look, then turned his attention and his gun back to the dog.

I shouldn't have, but I jumped the cruel bugger. Daisy took me close, and next thing I was rolling on the ground with him.

He was big. And angry.

Gave me a thumping before Dad arrived.

'Pull your heads in,' said Dad, dragging us apart. 'What the hell's going on?'

The farmer explained.

Dad was pretty ropeable when he got the gist.

Farmer wouldn't pay us. Wouldn't even give me a cold rag for my blood nose.

'You dopey idiot,' said Dad after we rode off. 'You know how farmers are with old dogs. What got into you?'

I didn't say anything.

In the distance we heard a single gunshot. Daisy and Jimmy both dropped their heads.

We rode on in silence.

After a couple of miles, Dad started up again.

'Going after a bloke twice your size,' he said. 'And a landowner at that.'

He looked at me and nodded.

'I'm proud of you, son,' he said.

3

Rest of that trip was good. Mostly on account of me keeping my trap shut about the war.

Dad forgave me for losing our pay. Said it was worth it. Said at least the dog would have known at the end that someone was on his side.

I stared into the campfire and kept quiet. When your old man's got the biggest heart in the district, best not to go on about it.

We did another job on the way back. Fixed up an old well at an abattoir. Manager thought it was dry, but it was just clogged. Dad knew in his bones there was water down there.

We got paid for that one so we were happy. Made an early start home the next morning. Daisy and Jimmy at a trot, all of us chipper as anything. Dad even had a bit of a whistle, which he hadn't done since Mum died.

Then we reached town and saw the hearse outside the pub.

Two coffins. An army hat on each one.

Empty coffins of course. The bodies were still over there, on some foreign battlefield. Army couldn't bring them back. Too hard to find the bits, probably.

Dad swore, which wasn't his style.

He went into the pub to make enquiries. While he was in there, a group of women and girls in funeral clothes came down the main street.

One of them was Joan. Her mother was with her.

I got off Daisy, to show respect and so Joan's mum could see I had manners.

A horrible thought hit me. Was one of the coffins for Joan's dad?

As Joan went past, I blurted it out.

'Is your dad all right?' I said.

Joan stopped, uncertain. Her mother gave her a sharp push to keep her moving.

'Major Prescott is fine,' said Mrs Prescott as she signalled to Joan to keep walking down the street. 'He's dispensing medicine in Egypt.'

The other women looked at me in a not very friendly way.

'So, Francis,' said one. 'What about your father?'

'Pretty right, thanks,' I said. 'He's in the pub.'

The women made disgusted noises as they walked off. I should have gone after them, explained they'd got it wrong. But I didn't. Joan was glancing back at me and I didn't want to get her into more strife.

When Dad came out of the pub, his face was dark. He paused by the hearse and touched both the coffins.

'Who are they?' I said.

'Ron and Nobby Shanks,' muttered Dad. 'Those mongrel Huns and Turks need a talking to.'

It was my day for saying stupid things.

'Thought you reckoned this was some other idiots' war,' I said.

Dad gave me a look. I was glad the bucket was in the back of the rig.

'They've killed two of my mates,' said Dad. 'So now it's personal.'

Poor Dad looked pretty gutted. But I couldn't help thinking about the bright side.

'That mean we'll be going?' I said.

Dad looked at me. He looked at the coffins. Then he swore and went back into the pub.

I waited with Daisy and Jimmy. Couple of blokes came out and took the hearse away.

When Dad came out again, quite a while later, he was staggering a bit. He pulled me roughly towards him and cupped my face in his hands.

He hadn't done that for years.

'I promised your mother,' he said in a beery voice. 'I promised her that you and me wouldn't go till you're old enough. End of story.'

He dropped his hands and we looked at each other.

'What's old enough?' I said.

Dad thought about this while he dragged himself up on to Jimmy. I was hoping Mum hadn't put the official army figure on it.

She had.

'Eighteen,' said Dad.

On my sixteenth birthday I got up early.

Spent some time with Daisy, rehearsing what I was going to say to Dad. How Mum wouldn't mind if we went now. How she'd agree that if you're tall for your age, and mature enough not to smoke, you're ready to do your bit.

'And she'd understand about girls,' I said to Daisy. 'How you have to go to war to get one.'

Daisy probably didn't have a clue what I was talking about. But she could tell from my voice it was important. So she stopped trying to get her head into my pocket looking for apples.

I hoped Dad would agree it was important. Huns and Turks were giving our blokes a battering. Memorial services most weeks in the district. Four coffins, some of them.

'So what if I'm not eighteen,' I said to Daisy. 'I've got hair where it counts.'

Daisy didn't argue. She'd seen me having baths in creeks. She knew I was ready to do my bit.

Heading into the house, I saw something on the verandah table.

A little box, wrapped up all pretty with a ribbon.

Jeez, I thought, that's not from Dad.

I picked it up.

It wasn't from him, it was for him. His name on it. Curly writing I'd never seen before.

'Happy birthday, son,' said Dad, coming out of the kitchen with something wrapped in newspaper. That was more his style.

'Thanks, Dad,' I said, taking the horse brush I knew he'd got for me.

'Struth,' said Dad, grinning and staring at the flash little box. 'Happy birthday from a lady, eh?'

'It's for you,' I said.

He frowned. I knew why. Mum hadn't even been dead a year.

'You open it,' he said.

Inside the pretty little box there wasn't a present.

Just a feather. A white feather. No note, but we both knew what the message was.

Only blokes who weren't in the army got white feathers. Blokes who people thought should be in the army. Sometimes people couldn't tell the difference between a coward and a stubborn parent.

Dad's face when he saw the feather. Only time I'd seen him looking more crook was when the doctor told us Mum wasn't going to make it.

'That's not fair,' I said. 'They don't understand.'

Dad didn't say anything. Just stared at it. But his face. No way he was putting off going now.

I had a worrying thought.

'We're a team,' I said. 'You're not dumping me with the rellies in Perth.'

'No,' muttered Dad. 'I'm not.'

Dad didn't like Mum's folks. At the funeral they blamed him for Mum getting sick. They didn't say anything, but you could tell.

So that was it.

We said oo-roo to the neighbours, nailed the windows shut, saddled up Daisy and Jimmy, and went to Sydney to volunteer.

4

The recruiting officer frowned. Gave all four of us the once-over.

Daisy and Jimmy snorted. They could tell the recruiting officer wasn't crazy about them. He didn't seem that keen about me and Dad either.

Jeez, I thought. What if he doesn't take us?

I'd been keeping that worry buried for days on the ride to Sydney. But it was out now. The shameful life ahead for us if me and Dad didn't do our bit. Me dying a lonely old bachelor with no wife and kids. Not even knowing what a girl's skin feels like. Dad getting spat on in the pub and probably no more work.

'They're both good horses,' said Dad to the officer. 'Walers. Faster than they look.'

I was glad he said that. Honest truth was they didn't look that nimble. Jimmy was getting on.

Daisy was beautiful with her white face and feet, but she was a bit of a crook shape.

'Safest feet in the district,' I said to the officer, which was a bit rich given Daisy's personality, but the officer probably wouldn't be talking to people out Cudgegong way.

'Show me,' said the officer.

The army camp had some jumps set up. Pretty tough ones. Barbed wire. Ditches full of mud. Not ordinary mud, army mud.

Dad went first.

I knew Jimmy'd be right, as long as he didn't get out of breath. He was more your slow and steady horse, Jimmy. Go all day at his own pace.

He was fine. Dad got him through.

Then it was my turn.

'You can do it, mate,' I murmured into Daisy's ear as we galloped at the first jump. She could be as cantankerous as a sack of chooks if she set her mind to it, so that was my way of saying please.

Daisy was a champ that day. She might have looked a bit rough, but she went over those jumps like an angel. She probably wasn't keen to see my miserable face for the next sixty years if she didn't.

'Right-o,' said the officer when we rode back. 'They're both army property now. You blokes get a medical.'

Me and Dad looked at each other.

Jimmy and Daisy were in. Now it was up to us.

The army doctor was impressed by my private parts, I could tell.

Not just the hair. I could also tell he'd noticed how that region was completely free of all fungal growths.

He didn't have a problem with my teeth either, or my feet, or my eyes.

Just my chest.

'Breathe in again,' he said.

I did, sticking my chest out like a scrub turkey with a mozzie bothering it.

'Just under the regulation minimum,' said the army doctor, looking at his tape measure.

I knew what that meant. Too skinny.

'Best of three,' I said to him, holding my arm out for an arm-wrestle.

The doctor didn't take up the offer. But he sort of smiled to himself.

'You've got the height,' he said. 'Couple of army feeds'll fill you out.'

He stamped my form.

'You're in,' he said. 'Welcome to the glorious crusade of the honourable and righteous against the dark pernicious forces of evil.'

'Thanks,' I said.

'Don't thank me,' he said. 'Not till you've been there and come back with everything still attached.'

Dad was in like Flinders fence-posts too. His back was good that day.

We took our forms to the recruiting officer so he could sign us up and arrange for the army to buy Jimmy and Daisy.

'Ages?' said the officer, checking the forms.

Me and Dad looked at each other. This was what we'd been worried about.

'Ages of the horses,' said the officer.

'Daisy's six,' I said, relieved. 'Jimmy's twelve.'

Soon as I said it I knew I shouldn't have.

'Army doesn't take horses over ten,' said the officer.

'We're a team,' said Dad. 'All or nothing.'

The officer thought about this. I hoped he could see Dad was a bloke who meant what he said.

'Come on,' said an impatient voice in the queue behind us. 'The Huns and Turks'll get sick of waiting and pack it in.'

The officer sucked his teeth.

'Twelve's close enough for a good mount,' he said, writing something on the form.

He gave me another hard look.

'When were you born?' he said.

'Eighteen ninety-eight,' I said. 'May.'

That was the date I'd worked out would make me the official army age.

'Best subject at school,' said the officer, looking me in the eye, 'clearly not arithmetic. It's nineteen fifteen now. The correct number of years ago would have been eighteen ninety-seven.'

'That's what Frank meant,' said Dad. 'Eighteen ninety-seven.'

The officer looked at us both.

'Hey, you lot,' said the voice behind us. 'When you've finished your Country Women's Association meeting, we're getting old and dying back here.'

The officer signed Dad's form. He didn't sign mine. Just folded it and stuck it into my hand.

'Go to the end of the queue,' he said. 'If we're as slow as that whingeing blighter reckons, when you make it back here you'll be a year older.'

'How do you spell pharmacy?' I said to Dad.

'Search me,' said Dad.

He was lying on his army bed, staring at the roof of the tent. He'd been doing it most nights since training started. Probably thinking about Mum.

Worrying about what she'd think of us being in the military.

Lucky it was a big tent. About ten other blokes in there. One of them helped out with the spelling.

'Ta,' I said.

Blokes of all types in the army. Even smart martins who'd been to university.

'What you writing?' said Dad.

I explained it was a letter to Joan. Letting her know what I was up to. We hadn't said goodbye to many people, Dad hadn't wanted to.

'I'm sending it care of the pharmacy,' I said. 'That way she might get it before her mother sees it.'

'Good thinking,' said Dad.

He went quiet again. I could see he was back to thinking about Mum.

I got up from my bed and went over to him.

'She'd understand,' I said. 'If she'd seen that feather she would.'

Dad didn't say anything for a bit. When he did, his voice was quiet.

'She does understand,' he said. 'I've talked to her about it.'

I stared at him. I'd had natters with Mum myself a couple of times, in dreams. All she'd wanted to talk about was keeping the birds off her veggie patch.

'What did she say?' I asked Dad.

'Private stuff,' he said. 'But one thing she wants me to tell you. She loves you, but she doesn't want to see you for a very long time.'

I thought about that.

'Right-o,' I said.

Poor Mum, she didn't have to worry. I wasn't planning on making a visit any time soon. What I was planning was a life with Joan.

A very long life.

5

Top clobber they gave you in the Light Horse.

Boots, hat with a feather, the lot. And the kit, quality stuff. Rifle, bayonet, even spare shoes for Daisy and Jimmy.

Training was tough. For Daisy and Jimmy too. Lot of standing around for them while we did shooting practice. Army reckoned we had to get them used to the sound of gunfire, and we only had two months to do it.

Daisy wasn't amused.

'Who broke this ammo box?' said the gunnery sergeant angrily.

I gave Daisy a look. That's all I needed, her being sent home for treading on army property.

Luckily the sergeant let it go, and as it turned out I was pretty all right at the shooting side of things.

'Cheeky blighter,' said Dad, peering at my target.

The targets were sheets of roofing tin with blokes painted on them. I'd got six hits, Dad had only got three.

'Mother's son, you are,' muttered Dad.

Mum was a crack shot. She used to win heaps of dolls at fairs. Not to mention keep the birds off the veggie garden, permanent.

The bloke next to me and Dad, he knew how to handle a gun too. Ten shots on target, all in the head. He was a few years older than me and dead-set full of himself.

'Too easy,' he said. 'Be better with moving targets. Army should ship some Turk prisoners back.'

Me and Dad swapped a glance. The bloke's name was Johnson. Angry eyes, black moustache. Looked like the sort of bloke who'd flatten the umpire with his bat if he was given out.

'Bush pigs'd do,' said Johnson. 'They look like Turks.'

I ignored him. Concentrated on squinting down the barrel, squeezing the trigger gently like Mum taught me.

'Letter for you,' said Dad a few weeks later.

He pointed to the envelope on my bed. Gave me a wink.

I was tuckered out after a long day on the training field, but I ripped that envelope open in record time.

It was from Joan.

Dear Frank

I was sad we didn't get to say goodbye. But I think I understand.

This is just to say good luck over there. Look after yourself. Specially your feet and armpits and the rest.

When you get there, home will probably seem a long way away. But we're thinking of you all and we're proud of you all.

Your friend,

Joan.

ps. Say g'day to your dad and Daisy for me.

There was something else inside the envelope. I fished it out.

A cough lozenge.

I must have been grinning like a kid. Dad gave me another wink. Some of the other blokes in our tent were chuckling.

I wasn't embarrassed. Or tuckered out any more. If you'd shown me fifty Turks, I'd have taken them on single-handed.

Big parade the day before we sailed.

Right through the middle of Sydney. Huge crowds. Felt good, up there on Daisy, complete strangers waving like they loved us.

But then I started thinking. Some of them, when they weren't carrying on like grandparents leaving to go back to Ireland, were probably sending white feathers to blokes who didn't deserve it.

I had a quick squiz at Dad next to me.

He and Jimmy looked like they were enjoying it heaps.

Two women were throwing flowers, great handfuls of them. Must have worked in a flower shop. Or an undertaker's joint.

I gave them a wave.

And froze.

Behind them, face shaded by a hat, was Mum.

Of course it wasn't her, but it was her dead-set double.

Dad saw her too. He was twisted round in the saddle, looking at her, drinking her in, when it happened. Jimmy stepped on a bunch of flowers, his foot slid and I saw a tendon go in his leg.

Dad felt it.

'Oh no, mate,' Dad said to Jimmy. 'That was my fault.'

Poor Jimmy was limping.

I leant over and gave him a rub. On the way to the docks I said a prayer, which I usually only did when I had a bet.

Please, I said silently. Make it a quick recovery, no officers involved.

Officers got involved.

Wouldn't let Jimmy on the boat.

'Fair go,' I said. 'He's a volunteer, like the rest of us.'

A sergeant yelled at me for mouthing off.

'Simple pulled tendon,' said Dad. 'Be right before you know it. Ask any of these blokes.'

The blokes around us all nodded. The sergeant threatened to put us all on a charge.

One of the regiment vets examined Jimmy.

'Three months before this one's right,' he said to the quartermaster. 'Unfit for military duty. Sorry, trooper.'

For a sec I thought Dad was going to fight them all. But the vet took Dad aside and had a quiet word to him. When he'd finished, Dad had calmed down.

I wasn't calm. I'd heard what could happen. In the army, if a horse was unfit, they got rid of it. What was Dad gunna do?

What he did was save Jimmy's life.

He requested compassionate leave. Four hours.

The sergeant glared at Dad. But requests like that had to be passed on to the commanding officer, army rules.

Word came back.

Granted.

It was hard, saying goodbye to Jimmy. I knew it'd be even harder for Dad.

'Oo-roo, Jimmy,' I said. 'See you down the track, mate.'

I could tell how upset Jimmy was. He and Daisy blew air on each other for a bit, then Jimmy gave some ship's stores on the dock a good hosing. A little something for the army to remember him by.

Dad took Jimmy to the railway station. Used all the money the army paid him for Daisy. Sent Jimmy up to a mate's property near Walgett.

That's the sort of bloke Dad was. If a horse does the right thing by you, he reckoned, you do the right thing by them.

'My mate Boney does a bit of horse-breeding,' said Dad when he got back from the station. 'Jimmy might get lucky.'

We all grinned, but I could see how cut up Dad was.

Why didn't I offer him Daisy and put in for a new horse myself in Egypt?

Dad wouldn't have come at it. A bloke's horse is his horse. Plus he knew what a handful Daisy could be if it wasn't me on her.

After we boarded the ship, the sergeant, who was impressed by what Dad had done, bought him a beer.

'Don't fret, mate,' he said to Dad. 'Plenty of horseflesh where we're going. Quite a lot of it still on four legs.'

Dad managed a chuckle. Which was a pretty impressive effort, considering.

Later, as we unpacked our kit for our first night on board, there was something nagging at me.

'What did that army vet say to you? I asked Dad. 'He calmed you down a treat.'

Dad looked like the question had caught him off balance.

'Can't say,' he replied. 'Official Secrets Act.'

I wasn't sure if he was joking.

'I can keep a secret,' I said.

'Nothing to write home about,' said Dad. 'Vet just reminded me that this war's bigger than one bloke and one horse.'

I knew Dad had never told me anything except the truth my whole life.

But there was something in his voice that made me wonder if this might be a first.

I wasn't sure whether to push it or not.

'Righty-o,' said Dad. 'Young legs, top bunk. Night, Frank.'

'Night, Dad.'

I let it go.

Had other things to think about. Joan, for a start. And wondering what it would look like when a bullet hit a bloke who wasn't made of tin.

6

Boat trip wasn't pretty. Hundreds of troopers and hundreds of horses crammed below decks. Six weeks of it.

There were some miserable creatures down there.

Horses and blokes.

We blokes chucked our guts for the first few days. But we all agreed it was worth it. Biggest adventure of our lives. Seeing the world. Doing our bit. Copping the glory.

Plus some of the blokes made friends with the nurses.

'You all right?' said Dad as we swabbed the bunk deck for the twentieth time.

'Nothing to it,' I said. 'Bit of vomit-mopping. Good practice for when Joan and me own a pub.'

It was harder for the horses. They didn't have medals to look forward to, or letters from home.

Most of the other horses were in a state on account of the ship rolling and plunging. Some were so bruised and lathered up they had to be put in slings and hoisted off the deck.

Not Daisy.

She was staggering a bit, but calm and balanced. Like she'd thought the whole thing through and accepted how it was.

When she saw us, course she let us know she didn't love it. Put her ears back and flared her nostrils and tried to stamp on our feet like they were going out of style. I explained I couldn't personally get us there any quicker because I wasn't the captain, but she just gave me the eye.

I didn't blame her. Nor did Dad.

'We volunteered,' said Dad as we brushed her. 'She didn't.'

He was right. Daisy and me were best mates, but sometimes on that voyage she probably felt like she was just a loyal creature being dragged along as part of some malarkey.

Plus there was her daughter. A two-year-old on a sheep property out west. Who probably didn't even know her mum was off to war.

Looking at Daisy I marvelled at her.

If she wanted to put her foot through her lunch bucket, that was all right with me.

Some of the horses didn't make it.

Ones down on the third level copped it worst. Hot as hell down there. Damp and dark. Fresh air scarce as French perfume.

Pneumonia, some of them.

Daisy was on the middle level and we got her up on deck for exercise as often as we could.

One day, halfway round the deck mats, we heard a splash.

I went to the railing for a squiz.

'Jeez,' I gasped.

There was a horse in the water. Not thrashing and struggling, just lying still. Slowly sinking into the greeny-grey depths.

Another splash. Another horse.

I realised what was happening. The vets were sliding dead horses out of a loading bay in the side of the ship.

Seven of them.

Shook the blokes bad. It would, seeing your horse dumped at sea. Seeing it die on dry land is bad enough.

I went back to Dad and Daisy.

'Second lot this week,' said Dad.

'Don't let Daisy see,' I said.

We didn't. But I reckoned she knew.

Nights were worst. Complete blackout in case German warships spotted us.

Bloke lit a match one time to put ointment on his feet. Nice bloke, my age, name of Otton. Knew hundreds of songs, which helped pass the time.

Sergeant put him on a charge.

They used to pick on us young troopers.

'How can the Huns see us down here?' said Otton. 'My teapot's got more portholes than this tub.'

'I'm not charging you for the blackout offence,' said the sergeant. 'I'm charging you for the gawd-awful singing.'

'Jeez,' said Otton after the sergeant had gone. 'Any more of this and I'm joining the Turks.'

Johnson, the sharpshooter who wanted live Turks for target practice, grabbed Otton by the throat.

'Say that again,' said Johnson, 'and you're a goner.'

'It was a joke,' I said to Johnson, trying to pull them apart.

'Hyperbole,' said Otton.

Johnson scowled. I knew how he felt. I didn't have a clue what a hyperbole was either. Judging from their frowns, neither did most of the other blokes.

Johnson threw himself on to his bunk.

Otton gave me a grateful wink.

'What's a hyperbole?' I said to him.

Otton shrugged.

'Dunno,' he said. 'I just like the word.'

I nodded. Me and Dad were self-educated too.

'Hey, Mr Ballantyne,' said Otton to Dad. 'You read the paper. What's a hyperbole?'

'It means go to bloody sleep,' said Dad. 'All of you.'

Sleeping was hard with the heat and with blokes muttering and with things crawling on you. But you got used to it. Had to. Couldn't go six weeks without a kip.

One night I woke up. Somebody was shaking me.

'You're talking in your sleep,' said Dad's voice in my ear.

'What was I saying?' I mumbled.

'You were calling out to Joan,' said Dad. 'Something about ointment.'

'Did the other blokes hear?' I said.

'Yes,' said about six voices. 'Now go back to sleep, you mongrel.'

I couldn't. After about an hour, I went up on deck. It was just getting light. Gold on the horizon.

I stared.

Was that land up ahead? Or just cloud?

I heard footsteps behind me. Thought it was the sergeant. Only sentries were meant to be up here at night, but I didn't care.

It was Dad.

'Can't you sleep?' he said.

'Don't want to,' I said. 'Case I yell more stuff out. Other blokes'll think I'm scared, going on about surgical supplies.'

Dad squinted at the horizon.

It was definitely land.

'Every bloke on this ship is scared,' said Dad. 'Ones who say they aren't are lying. Nothing wrong with being scared. Comes with the job.'

'Are you scared?' I said to him.

Dad didn't say anything for a bit. Kept looking at the horizon. The gold was turning red.

He turned to me and nodded.

7

Egypt was foreign, but the weather was Australian.

Heat and dust. Flies I reckoned I'd met before in Dubbo.

At the dock they put us on trains. Horses in open carriages, blokes in seats.

We didn't stay in our seats long. Hung out the windows getting an eyeful.

We were back on dry land, so we loved it. Crowds, markets, some very impressive piles of bricks, exotic pong of strange tucker.

Train went slow out of the city, so we got an eyeful of something else too.

Local horses doing it tough.

Real tough.

Local blokes were excavating a ditch. Using the poor nags to drag rocks and dirt. Me and Dad had seen mistreated horses, but nothing like this.

Poor blighters hadn't had a decent feed in weeks. Bones in gunnysacks. They could hardly stand.

One couldn't. Dropped to its knees. Bloke went crook at it with a whip. Another bloke slashing at it with a cane.

The troopers next to me at the window started yelling at them.

'Come on,' said Johnson, swinging his leg out the window. 'Let's sort those mongrels out.'

I was with him. You don't treat animals like that.

Next thing a sergeant had his face in ours.

'Anyone leaves this train,' said the sergeant, 'they're on the next boat home.'

We all thought about this. Stepped back from the window.

Dad pulled me into my seat.

'I know how you feel,' he said. 'Back home we'd take those clowns round the back of the pub and give 'em a lesson in animal husbandry. But this isn't back home. We're visitors here. They do things their way, we do things ours.'

I didn't say anything. I was still staring out the window, watching the cane rise and fall.

'This lot aren't the enemy,' said Dad. 'If the Huns and Turks hadn't come in knocking the place about, these blighters'd probably have more tucker for their animals.'

I pulled my eyes away from the window.

Dad knew stuff, so he was probably right.

But still.

The camp they took us to was huge. Stuck out in the desert. I couldn't see a single pyramid, sphinx or battlefield in any direction.

Tents to the horizon. Horse lines longer than our main street at home.

'Jeez,' muttered Dad. 'They'll need some water for this lot.'

Some of the troopers were drilling a well. Wrong spot, we could see.

Daisy could too. She stamped her feet and tossed her head like she did sometimes when humans were being dopes.

'Go and show 'em,' said Dad, giving me a nudge.

The blokes drilling weren't water monkeys like me and Dad, so it wasn't their fault.

'Best to read the scrub,' I explained to them. 'In parched country like this it shows you where the water is.'

'Engineer sergeant showed us where the water is,' said one of the troopers. 'And he can dock pay, so we're listening to him.'

I climbed on a pile of crates and took a squiz.

Otton and a couple of grease-smeared troopers climbed up too.

'Look for the scrub patterns,' I said, pointing.

The troopers were both frowning, not convinced.

'Takes experience,' Otton told them, tapping his nose and looking at the wrong patch of scrub.

'Takes the mickey more like,' said one of the other troopers.

'You four,' roared a voice. 'Off those crates.'

We got down.

A large engineer sergeant was looking like he was about to burst his pipes.

'Are you part of this deployment?' he growled at me.

'No, sergeant,' I said. 'Just arrived.'

'Congratulations,' said the engineer sergeant. 'You're on your first charge.'

'Fair go, sarge,' said Otton. 'He's a professional. Got a degree in Water Location and Advanced Well Insertion from Sydney Uni. What if he's right?'

The engineer sergeant gave me and Otton a long look. Then he turned to the troopers in the deployment.

'You blokes hit water yet?' he said, pointing to the drill rig. 'Bosworth? Lesney?'

The two blokes who'd been up on the crates with us shook their heads.

'And you reckon this new chum knows better than me?' said the engineer sergeant.

Bosworth and Lesney both hesitated, then shook their heads again.

Otton was nodding.

The engineer sergeant narrowed his eyes and gave Otton and me another very long look.

'Right-o,' he said. 'Prove it. If you hit water before dark, I'll drop the charge. If you don't, you're both in solitary for a week.'

After me and Daisy chose a spot, and the drill rig hit water, I showed the other blokes how to keep it flowing out of the sand by knocking holes in the bore tube.

'That's amazing,' said Lesney. 'I've been a news journalist for three years and I didn't know that.'

Bosworth snorted.

'You've been a trooper for three months,' he said, 'and you don't even know the Arabic for beer.'

Lesney and Bosworth wandered off, arguing.

'Thanks for getting that sergeant off my back,' I said to Otton.

'No sweat,' said Otton. 'You got Johnson off my back, so now we're commensurate.'

'Commensurate?' I said.

Otton grinned.

I got the gist.

The engineer sergeant came over.

'Effective as of now,' he said, 'you two are in the water deployment. I'll speak to your commanding officer.'

Otton wasn't delighted by the idea.

'Actually, Sarge,' he said, 'I can't work near water. My feet go mouldy. Plus it'd be a waste. I've got an advanced diploma in Military Strategy and Hand-To-Hand Combat from Tamworth Technical College.'

The sergeant wasn't impressed.

'The thing you've got an advanced diploma in, Trooper Otton,' he said, 'comes out the rear end of bulls.'

I put Daisy back on the line and went to find Dad.

He was unpacking in our troop's tent.

'I'm in the water deployment,' I said. 'I've been co-opted.'

Dad grinned.

'Two days in Egypt,' he said, 'and you're speaking army.'

'There's a spot for you too,' I said. 'Otton doesn't want it. They'd bust a gut to have you.'

Dad shook his head.

'Not this time, mate,' he said. 'This one's yours.'

I stared at him. Dad and me were a team. The water unit needed his experience as much as it needed mine.

More.

What was going on?

'Comes a time,' said Dad, 'when a bloke's got to strike out on his own.'

I agreed, but not yet.

Back home, after the war, that's when I'd be striking out on my own, with Joan.

'Let's find the blacksmith,' said Dad. 'I want him to take a look at Daisy's feet. She'll keep going forever, but you've got to make sure her shoes are right.'

I knew that.

Why was he telling me that?

Why wasn't he doing something much more important?

Getting himself a new horse.

8

A week later the penny dropped.

I'd been out for an early morning gallop with Daisy. Just a quick one. She was still getting her sand legs after the boat trip. When we got back, the news was all over the camp.

An order had come through. Some of the Light Horse outfits, including ours, were getting back on a boat to fight in the Dardanelles.

On foot.

Leaving the horses behind.

'Where are the Dardanelles?' I said to Dad.

'Arse-end of Turkey,' said Dad. 'Pommy generals started an invasion and lost the plot. Me and some of the other blokes are going over to give 'em a hand. Reinforce our blokes already there.'

'I'm going too,' I said.

'No you're not,' said Dad.

'Yes I am,' I said. 'What'll Joan's parents think if I pike out?'

Me and Dad were face-to-face, so worked up we didn't see the engineer sergeant come over.

'I'm going,' I yelled.

'No you're not,' yelled Dad.

'I'll second that,' said the sergeant. 'And that's an order.'

I was done for. I might have got round Dad, but not the army as well.

'Horses need you here,' said Dad. 'They'll die of thirst with these clowns.'

The engineer sergeant made Dad and me shovel horse poop for the rest of the day. But he didn't tell Dad he was wrong.

After a lot of shovelling, I calmed down.

'The horses need you just as much,' I said to Dad. 'Why aren't you staying?'

Dad just shovelled in silence.

I didn't get it. Dad was in the Light Horse. Why did he want to go off to some lump of rock and fight on foot?

Then I did get it.

The white feather.

The bloody mongrel white feather.

After that I didn't try to stop Dad.

Wanted to?

Course I did.

But I could see he didn't have any choice, so I stuck by him. He'd done that for me all my life. Now it was time for me to do it back.

That's what I told myself, standing there in the first light as Dad and the other blokes got on the train for the docks.

'Oo-roo, Dad,' I said.

'Good on you, son,' said Dad quietly.

I cupped his face in my hands. Hadn't planned to. Just did.

'Watch your arse over there,' I said. 'If you cop one, Daisy'll be ropeable. She's hard enough on a bloke's feet as it is.'

Dad smiled, touched me on the cheek, and got on the train.

'Say g'day to Mum for me,' I called.

Soon as I said it, I wished I hadn't. In case he misunderstood.

But Dad smiled and waved.

I watched the train choof off into the distance.

Typical Egyptian desert dawn.

Red as all get out.

Rumours started a few weeks later. Army censors had been trying to stop them for months, but word finally trickled through.

Dardanelles was a dunny. Turks up on the high ground, our lot copping it down below.

I tried not to worry about Dad.

Over the next few months I tried to stay chipper, waiting for proper news. Worked hard in the water deployment. Wrote letters to Joan. Waited patiently for her next letter to make it to Egypt.

Daisy helped take my mind off things. Early every morning we did a long gallop out in the desert.

One time a couple of officers on horseback pulled us over.

'G'day trooper,' said one. 'Nice horse.'

'Yes, sir,' I said, trying not to be too friendly.

An officer could requisition a trooper's mount if he liked the look of it. This bloke obviously knew horses. Not like the British cavalry officers who sniggered when they saw Daisy, just on account of her being a bit wonky.

'Fine waler,' said the officer.

Suddenly I recognised him. The army vet who'd calmed Dad down at the docks in Sydney.

'Permission to ask something, sir,' I said.

'Go ahead, trooper,' he said.

I reminded him about Dad and Jimmy.

'What did you say to my father that day, sir?'

The vet swapped a glance with the other officer.

'We knew things in the Dardanelles were getting difficult,' he said. 'And that some of the Light Horse reinforcements would be required there on foot. I told your father not to fret about his mount as he probably wouldn't be needing one for a spell.'

I took this in.

'Thanks,' I said.

After the officers rode on, I got off Daisy and sat on the sand.

I thought about Dad. What he'd done. Saved me from being a foot-slogger in the Dardanelles. How he'd never stopped looking out for me, ever. Not even when his heart was broken.

I sat thinking for a long time, Daisy standing there shading me.

I wished I could thank Dad.

Tell him how much I loved him.

'Too late,' I said to Daisy. 'Too late now. I'll have to wait till he gets back.'

9

When the first blokes got back to our camp from the Dardanelles, we all just stared, Daisy included.

Walking ghosts.

I hadn't seen anything like it since I was little.

Back then Dad was working in a gypsum mine with his father.

Big collapse.

Mum and me rushed to the pit. Blokes were coming out, the few that made it. Pale with dust and shock. Silent.

Grandad wasn't with them.

Dad didn't talk for two days after that.

This time the brass didn't want our Dardanelles blokes to talk at all, permanent.

But the first ones back did.

They reckoned most of the fighting in the Dardanelles was on a strip of rock called Gallipoli.

Abattoir, they reckoned.

Our blokes got slaughtered.

Light Horse lost hundreds. Some of the best horsemen in Australia, dead on their feet not five yards out of the trenches. Some got a few steps more, blown into pieces so small they didn't even have a grave.

Dad included.

That's what they said.

But I didn't give up hope.

Mayhem over there, that's what they also said. Lines of communication in tatters. Men ending up in the wrong regiment, uniforms in shreds, fumbling through their wallets trying to find their own names.

So I didn't give up hope.

Otton helped. Made sure our regimental sing-songs had plenty of cheery ballads.

Daisy helped too. Stuck with me, her head on my shoulder.

Until I saw it.

Dad's name.

On the dead list.

I wanted to be in the ground like Dad was.

So I tried to do what we did after Mum died. Keep working. Keep busy. Let water wash away the pain.

I found an old Arab well. Hundreds of years old, they reckoned. Been dry for decades. Fifty feet deep and the bottom wasn't even damp.

Dad had told me about wells like this.

Lined with stone, ancient style. The stones bleed minerals. Clog themselves up. Their strength is their weakness, that's what Dad reckoned.

Hours I was down there, looking for water.

Scraping and hacking at those mongrel stones. Stabbing them. Clawing at them. Yelling at them.

Nothing weak about those stones. Hard as a Turk's heart those stones were.

I knew there was water, I could feel it close. But it didn't come. So I stopped waiting for some dopey liquid to make me feel better.

I decided to give up on water.

Try something else.

'Ballantyne, here's your delivery.'

Trooper Johnson barged into the quiet spot where I was sitting with Daisy cleaning my rifle.

I was glad to see him. Or rather I was glad to see

what he'd got with him. A bundle of rags, which he dropped at my feet.

I handed him the money. A month's pay.

Johnson took it, then stared at Daisy.

'Jeez,' he said. 'She's ugly.'

Rude tosser. That wasn't on. Insulting a horse who was in mourning and too sad to give him one in the privates.

I didn't say anything, just stood up and swung one into his jaw.

He dropped.

My hand felt like I'd fractured it.

Johnson picked himself up. I put my fists up, waiting for him to come at me. But he just leaned against the shed and spat some blood.

'It's just a mongrel horse,' he said, glowering at me. 'You need locking up.'

Otton appeared as Johnson walked away.

'What happened?' he said.

'He insulted Daisy,' I said.

Otton stared at me. Then at Daisy. Then grinned.

'You gotta admit, Frankie,' he said. 'She's not the prettiest girl on the line.'

Death wish, that bloke.

I took a step towards him.

'All right,' he said. 'I'm sorry. Jeez. Touchy. What did Johnson want, anyhow?'

I picked up the bundle of rags and carefully unwrapped it. Nestled in the bundle was the most vicious weapon I'd ever seen.

'Beautiful, isn't it?' I said.

Otton stared.

It was a bayonet. A regulation-issue bayonet. But different. Instead of a smooth blade, it was edged with jagged metal teeth.

Razor sharp.

'Johnson made it,' I said. 'Hobby of his.'

Otton couldn't take his eyes off it.

'He'll make one for you,' I said. 'Only nine quid.'

'Me?' said Otton. 'No way. I'm an apprentice auctioneer. I sing at weddings on weekends. Thing like that isn't in my province or my dominion.'

I shrugged.

'Jeez,' said Otton, still staring at the bayonet. 'Those Turk mongrels that killed your dad. In and twist with that and they'll be dog meat.'

He gave me a nervous glance, as if he thought he'd gone too far.

He hadn't.

10

It was personal now.

I wanted those Turks and Huns bad. I wanted to irrigate the desert with them. I wanted to kill so many the local farmers would be growing blood oranges, permanent.

Daisy felt the same, I could tell.

So did a lot of the other blokes. Their dead mates at Gallipoli were counting on them.

All we wanted was to get started.

Army had other ideas. Training, months of it. Including on Christmas Day and my seventeenth birthday.

'Blow this for a waste of sweat,' I said as we oiled our saddles and bridles for the thousandth time. 'We should be training on the job, like the blokes over in France. They'll be getting stuck into those mongrels now.'

'Dying of boredom in trenches, more like,' said Otton, rubbing ointment into his feet for the thousandth time. 'Sitting around waiting to be attacked. Lucky if they get the occasional skirmish or contretemps.'

'That's right,' said a passing troop sergeant, flicking dust off Otton's bridle. 'A trench is no place for you blokes. Army's got bigger plans for you. Elite mobile desert fighting force, you blokes. If you can stop your gear falling to bits, that is.'

Mobile desert fighting force.

I liked the idea of that.

'When do we start?' said Lesney.

'You blokes'll be the first to know,' said the troop sergeant.

Daisy snorted.

The sergeant stopped and frowned.

'No, come to think of it,' he said, 'this is the army so you probably won't.'

We even did battle practice in our time off.

Horse Olympics, we called it. Races. Tug-o-wars. Horseback wrestling and the like. And one very special event.

It was Otton's idea.

'Very popular at country weddings,' he said.

'After a sheila's caught the bridal bouquet, all the blokes have a joust for it. Lucky winner cops a kiss from the sheila. Or her mum.'

I tried not to think about the awful possibility of having to kiss Joan's mother at our wedding.

In the Egyptian desert there was a shortage of bridal bouquets. Wasn't much of a floral nature in general. So we rigged something else up. A pair of knotted long johns.

Drew a face on it.

A Turk head.

We dangled it from a palm tree and two blokes on horseback squared up equal distances from it. When the whistle blew they rode at it full pelt, each trying to hook the head on their bayonet.

Daisy was a legend at it.

The bayonets had tins of bully beef stuck on the end so nobody got hurt.

Not yet.

Then, at last, it was on.

We were playing pool in the local town with blokes from signals. We were winning, partly on account of them being distracted by a bunch of nurses, and partly on account of them being nervous when they heard that Otton had an

Advanced Diploma in Snooker from Tamworth Tech.

Signals blokes ran out of money, so they gave us info instead. Reckoned our air boys had spotted Turk troop build-ups. Great mobs of them.

We were so excited we couldn't sleep. Lay awake in our tent waiting for them to attack.

Didn't happen.

Pom infantry reported that even the small attacks had stopped.

We were confused.

Came up with various theories.

Lesney, who was planning to be a sports journo, reckoned it was on account of Turks and Huns not playing test cricket, so they didn't understand about sticking at something day after day after day.

Bosworth reckoned it was because the local Bedouin tribes were stealing the Turks' boots while they were asleep. Sometimes taking their feet as well if the laces were double-knotted.

Otton reckoned the whole thing was subterfuge. Or some word like that.

Few days later, on parade, our colonel put us straight.

'The enemy is building up its forces,' he said. 'Tens of thousands coming down from the north. Very important not to let them get organised.

Which is why we're now going on the offensive. Push them back to where they came from. Those that survive meeting us.'

A cheer roared across the parade ground.

Even the blokes who'd perfected the art of having a snooze while standing to attention were wide awake and chucking their hats in the air.

'At last,' I said to Dad under my breath. 'We're going after the mongrels.'

11

Then things moved fast.

Our orders were to head north-east into the desert, up towards Palestine, and engage the enemy. Us and some British cavalry.

We mustered by moonlight. Formed up and rode out at dawn in mounted columns. Big mob of us.

We were hungry for it.

Long ride. Sixteen hours. Sand shifting under Daisy's feet the whole time, but she was rock solid.

Even when German planes machine-gunned us, she hardly flinched.

First air attack was early arvo. We learned quick smart what to do and what not to do. Watched a British cavalry troop gallop in clever patterns across the sand, making themselves moving targets.

Harder to hit was the idea.

Not so clever.

In five minutes they were history, blood-stained riding boots and scraps of thoroughbred scattered everywhere.

I held on tight to Daisy, so the other blokes wouldn't see me trembling.

By the time the Hun planes were back for a second go, we'd worked it out. If you stayed rock-still, the planes couldn't tell you from a sandstone outcrop or a dune shadow.

Daisy was a champ. As the planes came at us I was shaking like a windmill. If I'd been a horse, I'd have been bolting, or on my belly with my hooves over my eyes.

Not Daisy. Hardly a quiver.

I tried to make my breathing like hers, slow and easy. And for the rest of that day, whenever we heard the whine of a plane engine and the flapping of its canvas coming over the desert, we'd stop and breathe together, calm and still, like we were the same creature.

It was the bombs that did us in.

Last air attack of the day, the German mongrels hung out of their planes and chucked bombs at us. Still couldn't see us, but the shrapnel went every which way.

Cut our blokes and horses down like wheat.

Blokes I'd played snooker with. Had camp-fire sing-songs with.

Not Daisy, thank God. She scrambled to her feet.

I picked myself up and started breathing again.

'You all right?' I said to Otton and Bosworth and Lesney.

They nodded, eyes still wide with shock.

I knew how they felt.

We patched up our casualties as best we could. Loaded each wounded bloke ambulance-style on to his horse, arms and legs tied under its belly. Filled their horses' water bags from ours and sent them back to camp with an escort.

'Not much water left for us,' I muttered to Otton as we dug graves.

Otton nodded. He looked worried too.

Our column headed on into the desert. Vast sandy oceans, shimmering rocky plains, all dry as a pub on Sunday.

Otton tried to keep our spirits up with a few songs, but by the end of the afternoon we were out of water and not in good shape.

Daisy was sick with thirst.

She didn't stop, but some of the other horses did.

They couldn't help it, they weren't walers.

When they dropped, they dropped. Kneeled down first, then rolled over and just lay there, eyes staring at something far away. A nice grassy paddock with a dam probably.

Officers called the column to a halt. If we started losing horses, soon we'd be losing blokes too. You didn't last long on foot in those parts.

We dismounted and let the horses rest.

Big worry was that the Hun fliers had given the Turks our location. Enemy troops on their way. Watered-up and hungry for us.

None of the blokes said it, but we were all thinking the same thing. Few more hours without water, we'd be too weak to fight.

'Everyone got a bullet?' said Johnson.

Blokes in our troop all nodded.

Unwritten rule. No Light Horseman ever let himself be taken prisoner.

Ever.

Bosworth and Lesney were slumped next to their horses. Even Otton was sitting staring at the sand.

I decided to risk it. Daisy was still standing.

'Permission to scout for water, sir,' I said to a lieutenant.

He gave me a weary look. Thought I was being a comedian. Then he recognised me.

'Permission granted,' he said.

I swallowed the second last swig of water from my canteen. Gave the last mouthful to Daisy.

We set off. Filthy country. Sand, rock, nothing growing. Even the scorpions looked thirsty. We pushed on, hoping for a change in geography.

All we got was dusk.

Then darkness.

Then a desert fog.

'Dad'd have a smile if he saw this,' I said to Daisy. 'Hundreds of us back there dehydrating to death and now here's you and me blinded by very small drops of water.'

Daisy wasn't smiling. Nor was I. You couldn't drink mist. And just because you couldn't see the enemy, didn't mean they couldn't see you.

One sniper's bullet and Joan would never know what had happened to me. Never know what I really felt about her. The sort of feelings you can't put in a letter. Only in a whisper.

Me and Daisy headed slowly on through the swirling dark.

'Go easy,' I murmured, but Daisy knew what she was doing.

Suddenly she stopped.

I held my breath. Listening for the clink of Turkish rifle straps.

Nothing.

Then the fog drifted and in the moonlight I saw why Daisy had stopped. We were on the edge of a wadi. Sort of a deep, dry creek bed.

Sheer hundred-foot drop. Two more steps and we'd have been history.

'Thanks,' I whispered to her.

In filthy country a hundred-foot drop is a gift. If you can get down there without breaking your neck, you're a hundred feet closer to water.

There was water buried deep in that wadi, plenty for the whole column. Thanks to it, we got to the enemy late afternoon the next day.

Timing was good.

Through the binocs we could see the Turks having a water stop themselves. Clustered round a couple of old wells. Hundreds of the mongrels, so it was taking them a while.

'Jeez,' said Otton, staring at their artillery units. 'They've got some inordinately big guns.'

'Look at the gunners, but,' I said. 'All got their heads in the trough.'

Perfect time to charge. Every trooper knew it.

Stay mounted, gallop at them, do 'em before they even saw us coming.

I had my bayonet wrapped in a sock in my saddlebag, waiting.

The order came.

Dismount.

We couldn't believe it. We stayed mounted. I saw Johnson up the line, scowling and cursing.

The lieutenant glared at us.

'Dismount,' he repeated.

We didn't have any choice. Mounted infantry we were officially. Ride to the point of engagement, our orders said, then dismount and go at the enemy on foot.

Johnson wasn't the only bloke who was ropeable. And the horses weren't that happy either.

It got worse.

Some mug had to hold the horses. Each section of four blokes, one of us had to be the horse-holder. Stay back from the action. Keep the horses safe. So the other blokes could mount up when the fighting was over.

Our troop sergeant pointed at me.

'No,' I pleaded.

I looked at the other blokes in my section, begging.

They were a sorry mob that day. Lesney had the squirts. Bosworth had saddle rash. Otton was limping from all the times he'd parted company from his horse. I was the fittest bloke in the section.

None of them saw my pleading look. Couldn't take their eyes off the enemy.

I didn't blame them. I had it too. Turk-hunger.

'Ballantyne,' said the troop sergeant, jamming four sets of reins into my hands. 'You're the horse-holder.'

I shook my head.

Troop sergeant blew out his cheeks.

'You don't get it, do you sonny?' he said. 'This is orders from above.'

'What orders?' I said.

'On account of your nose for water,' said the troop sergeant. 'Orders are, it has to stay on your face at all times.'

The order to charge sounded.

Otton gave a sympathetic shrug. He and the others sprinted towards the Turks, bayonets drawn, yelling the war cries we'd learned in training, happy as dogs in dust.

I chucked the reins on to the sand.

If the other nags were like Daisy, they didn't even need a horse-holder.

The troop sergeant squared his shoulders.

'You disobeying an order?' he said.

I nodded.

The troop sergeant took a step closer.

'No you're not, sonny,' he said. 'I reckon you just didn't hear it. Listen careful this time. While I remind you what happens if you disobey an order in the face of the enemy.'

He held the business end of his rifle an inch from my head.

'Hearing improved?' he said.

I picked up the reins.

The troop sergeant moved on to the other horse-holders.

I stood with my horses, watching Turks being cut down by blokes whose fathers were still alive.

Fifteen months since I'd volunteered, and I still hadn't got close enough to give a Turk a haircut, let alone sign his family up for a pension.

Daisy was frustrated too. Waiting on the edge of that battle, air thick with screaming metal, she flared her nostrils and snorted.

'Don't worry,' I said to her. 'I'm not letting this happen again. Next time it's our turn.'

12

As we advanced towards Palestine, word got around.

The Turks were calling us desert ghosts.

Dune jackals.

Every time a Light Horse regiment came out of the desert haze, the Turks'd poop themselves. They couldn't believe our horses. Bred for outback work, our walers. Guts and stamina.

But even walers needed water, and you couldn't always find water in the desert, not even in the Holy Land.

So the Turks started making it harder. Defending their wells. Trenches, machine-guns, artillery with crack gunners.

Few weeks later, our next battle. Turks were dug in. Impossible to shift. Like our troop sergeant.

'Ballantyne,' he said, just like the time before. 'Horse-holder.'

Before I could say a word, he gave me the eye and patted his rifle.

Mongrel.

Daisy gave my elbow a nip.

She was right. I pulled my head in. No point getting shot by one of our own. But I wasn't taking this, not permanent. I wasn't missing out again.

I waited for the troop sergeant to move on.

As soon as he was distracted, I'd be going in.

The battle was noisier than a grand final. Our blokes were coming off worst.

Order came. Retire.

Suddenly I saw my chance. When blokes were pinned down, trying to retreat, you didn't wait for them to come to you, you took the horses to them.

'This is it,' I said to Daisy, crouching low on her neck. 'Our turn.'

We went in fast with the other three horses on a tight rein. Smoke, machine-gun fire, shell-bursts spraying sand.

Otton, Lesney and Bosworth were squatting in a shell hole, firing over each other's shoulders.

The Turk trenches were a hop and a skip away. Jam-packed full of the mongrels.

I could have gone for one right there.

Several.

But first I had to get my section mounted.

'Order's in,' I screamed at them, metal flying past in all directions. 'Retire.'

Wasn't the neatest mount-up. Lesney took one in the leg. Just flesh, far as we could see.

Otton and Johnson kept firing to give us cover. We got Lesney into the saddle and pointed him in the right direction.

'I'll catch up with you,' I said.

The others took off.

I wheeled Daisy round to get myself a Turk.

Smoke was thicker than a wheat-stubble burn-off. But I could see that most of the mongrels were still in their trenches.

Not all, but. Some were out and looking for bayonet practice. Which reminded me that mine, the special one, was still in my saddlebag.

I fumbled with the buckle.

No way was I going to pike out. I'd paid for that bayonet. Every razor tooth. It was for Dad.

I got the saddlebag open, but before I could get my hand in, a shell exploded close.

Real close.

One time, years before, I was slow getting my head out of a shaft when the charge blew. That was bad, but nothing like this.

Me and Daisy were covered with blood and God knows what else.

Oh Jeez, I thought. What have I done? What if some of this is hers?

I made myself think clearly. Daisy was still on her feet, so she couldn't be hurt too bad.

I got her out of there.

It was chaos. Some of our blokes from other sections had lost their horses. On the way out I saw a bloke stumbling around in the smoke, uniform half blown off. I didn't slow down, just scooped the bloke up. Dad would have been proud. He taught me how to grab livestock on the run. I got bronze once in the chook-snatching at the picnic races.

'Hang on tight, mate,' I said. 'Daisy'll get us back.'

The bloke didn't say anything. I glanced at him to see if he was wounded.

He wasn't wounded, he was a Turk.

We looked at each other, me with my arm round him. My first Turk, and I didn't have a spare hand to kill him.

I gripped Daisy with my knees. Let go of the reins. Reached into the saddlebag and found the bayonet.

Before I could use it, the smoke suddenly cleared and bang in front of us was barbed wire.

Daisy stopped in her tracks.

Me and the Turk went over her head.

Crashed on to the sand inches from the wire. Breath knocked out of me, but I managed to roll on top of the Turk and get the bayonet up to his neck.

He was gripping my wrist.

I was stronger. And riled.

'This is for Dad, you murdering mongrel,' I yelled at him.

He wasn't struggling or pleading or praying out loud. Just looking at me. And sort of wheezing.

He was even older than Dad. And his expression. Sad and disappointed and bewildered all at the same time.

Dad with the feather.

I imagined this mongrel at Gallipoli. Squeezing the trigger as Dad came out of the trench. Punching bullet after bullet into Dad's flailing body.

I closed my eyes and gripped the bayonet harder and tried to force it into his neck. I screamed at him so loud I could hear myself over the exploding shells.

But I couldn't do it.

13

I thought about leaving the Turk there on the battlefield, but I didn't.

He was a prisoner.

You didn't abandon prisoners. Rules said you took them into custody. So that's what I did.

It's what Dad would have done.

'Don't worry,' I said to Daisy as I tied the Turk's hands. 'He won't hurt you.'

She looked like she'd hurt him if she got the chance.

I dragged him up on to her back and we rode off with my arm round his neck.

After a bit we caught up with some Welsh infantry on the march. Judging by their sour mugs, they must have been ordered to retreat before they even got to the battle.

I rode up to one of their officers.

'Prisoner in your care, sir,' I said.

The officer looked at me. Looked at the Turk. Wasn't pleased to see either of us. But he ordered a couple of his blokes to take the Turk into custody.

The Turk gave me a look as they took him away. A grateful look.

I didn't want to see it.

After the officer had gone, some of the Welshies came over.

'Why didn't you just neck him?' said one.

'He was unarmed,' I said.

One of the other Welsh blokes pointed to the extra feed bags on Daisy.

'Nancy horse-holder,' he muttered to his mates. 'Lucky the horses need holding. Gives the cowards something to do.'

Infantry, they were always whingers, miserable plods.

I was tempted to sort that Taffy plod out. I didn't. Blokes on the same side punching each other was dopey. I just dismounted and looked the Taff hard in the eyes.

'My name's Francis Ballantyne,' I said. 'Come and see me after the war and we'll chew it over then.'

He glared at me. I didn't blink. Or give any sign that might lead a pea-brain Taff to think I was lacking in the guts department.

But somewhere inside me, tiny and trickling, was the worry that when it came to killing Turks maybe I was.

Back at camp I gave Daisy a proper wash-down.

Big relief. She was fine. But she let me know she wasn't crazy about wearing somebody else's blood and guts.

'Sorry,' I said. 'Putting you in it like that.'

She flicked her ears and kicked at my shins a bit, then calmed down and forgave me.

I dried her off and gave her a feed.

'Back in a tick,' I said.

Went to see how Lesney was.

'Came out clean,' said Lesney, patting the bandage on his leg. 'I've had worse from a news editor.'

'He's being stoic,' said Otton. 'It went close to something critical.'

'Yeah,' said Bosworth. 'His wallet.'

I didn't really feel like socialising, so I went back to Daisy.

Brushed her carefully, every inch. Just to be sure. Shrapnel could sit under the skin and go septic if you didn't spot it.

'Can I ask you something?' I said to her. 'Do you reckon I let Dad down today?'

She didn't understand all the words, but it felt good to get them out. Mum taught me it was easier to think about things when the words were out.

Daisy just kept chewing her feed. Egyptian straw was like that, lot of chewing, not much to swallow.

I knew how she felt.

'I'll go for a walk,' I said. 'Find you something better.'

'Jeez,' said a voice. 'I think I've cracked a knuckle.'

Johnson was heading towards us along the horse lines, grimacing and rubbing his fist.

I looked at him, startled.

We'd hardly spoken for months. Not since I'd cracked my knuckles on him.

'Couple of Taffys needed a talking to,' said Johnson. 'About who they call a coward.'

I stared at him.

'You didn't have to . . .' I said.

'No worries,' he said. 'You're a mad bugger, but you're not a coward.'

'Thanks,' I said doubtfully.

I still wasn't sure what he was doing here.

'I explained it to 'em,' said Johnson. 'How a coward's a bloke with an inability to kill anyone 'cause he was brought up wrong. Whereas you're just a choosy individual who's saving his first kill for a special occasion.'

I looked at him.

'Special occasion?' I said.

'Later tonight,' he said.

I still didn't understand.

'I can see you're disappointed by how things turned out today,' said Johnson. 'So I'm inviting you on a little hunting expedition.'

14

All us troopers were meant to get leave, regular.

Didn't happen.

When regiments were on the move, fighting a tough desert campaign, setting up a series of field camps, each one further north as we pushed the mongrel Turks back towards Turkey, there wasn't any leave.

Not official.

But field camps didn't have much in the way of fences and gates, so if you were up for it and gung-ho and desperate to avenge your dad, a bit of leave was possible.

Otton wasn't all that gung-ho. Plus he didn't need revenge. His dad died in a sheep-drenching accident that was entirely the fault of the sheep.

'If we're caught, we'll be shot,' said Otton, as me and him and Johnson rode out into the moonlit desert on our hunting expedition. 'It's as simple and categorical as that.'

'Shut it,' growled Johnson.

Johnson hadn't wanted Otton to come.

Otton had insisted.

'When a mate goes on a suicide mission,' Otton had said, 'you go with him.'

Johnson had scowled at that.

He was scowling even more now.

'If you haven't got the ticker,' he said to Otton, 'this is where you leave us. We're here to kill Turks. Face-to-face. Like men.'

'Why face-to-face?' said Otton nervously.

Johnson licked his lips.

In the moonlight his moustache was very black against his white teeth.

'Respect,' he said. 'No fun killing blokes if you don't respect them.'

Johnson rode on ahead. He said it was to scout for Turks. And so he wouldn't have to listen to Otton humming.

Otton rode close to me and Daisy.

'I know why you're doing this, Frank,' he said. 'You're doing it to impress that paramour of yours back home.'

I gave him a look. To remind him about Dad.

'There are more important reasons for killing Turks,' I said.

'Sorry,' said Otton.

'Anyway,' I said. 'I wouldn't call her a paramour. Unless that's a technical word for someone who doesn't answer letters.'

Otton sighed.

'How many times do I have to reiterate?' he said. 'You're being too impatient. The mail takes months each way.'

'I've been writing for a year and a half,' I said. 'I've had one letter from her, and that was back in Sydney.'

Otton thought about this.

'You sure she can read?' he said. 'I knew a sheila once, worked for a doctor, couldn't read or write a word. Had to draw pictures of malfunctioning body parts on the file cards.'

Before I could remind him that Joan had a scholarship, Daisy stiffened.

I wasn't sure why at first. Then I felt a breeze. And heard a rumbling in the distance.

Otton and I looked at each other.

Big guns?

Large numbers of Turkish troops in motor lorries?

Daisy stopped and sniffed the air.

There was something about the way she was trembling that made my guts tighten.

Then we saw what it was. Daisy was right.

This was worse than guns or troops.

Me and Dad had copped a few sandstorms out west in New South Wales. Bit of dust in the face and the odd airborne lizard.

This one was a hundred times worse.

As it howled towards us, the moonlight began to disappear. Soon I couldn't even see Daisy, and I was on her back.

'Get down flat,' I yelled at Otton through the howling sand. He was only a few feet away, but I didn't have a clue if he could hear me.

I stripped the gear off Daisy and tried to make her lie down. Wasn't easy. She was furious. Wanted to give that sandstorm a serious kicking.

I finally got her down and wrapped a blanket round her head. Dropped down next to her with the saddlecloth round mine and used the saddle as a windbreak.

Thought I got a glimpse of Otton doing the same.

I hoped so.

We were there for a long time.

I had plenty to do. Digging the sand away from us mostly, stopping it building up over our faces. And making sure we both got water when we needed it. Just small swigs from my canteen.

Did Otton have water? And Johnson?

Too late if they didn't.

I got close to Daisy's ear and tried to keep her spirits up. Told her a few things she might not know about our family. How upset Dad was when he had to sell her daughter. How he needed the money for Mum's funeral. How grateful we were to Daisy that Mum had a proper grave.

It was true, but it wasn't very cheery, so I sang Daisy a few songs. Not a total success. My mouth kept filling up with sand.

As the wind finally calmed down a bit, the swirling darkness lifted.

It was dawn.

I looked around for Otton. Couldn't see him or his horse.

The whole landscape had changed. Dunes the size of our troop ship, completely shifted.

And still shifting. Big gusts of wind flinging sand around like shrapnel.

I still couldn't see Otton. Until a small dune erupted and Otton's horse stood up and shook herself. Daisy went over and they nuzzled each other.

Then Otton's horse hosed on a pile of sand, which swore loudly. Otton staggered to his feet, coughing and spitting.

'You all right?' I said.

'That was the worst experience of my life,' croaked Otton. 'And I've had diphtheria.'

'Quiet,' growled a voice.

Johnson had come up behind us.

'Hear that?' he said.

Faintly, through the hissing wind, the sound of voices. Yelling, hysterical, panicked voices. You couldn't make out what they were saying. But then none of us spoke Turkish.

Johnson grinned.

'Good,' he said. 'They're in a state. They won't be expecting us.'

We heaved ourselves over a sand-blown ridge on our stomachs.

I gripped my rifle hard. This was it. I wasn't going to pike out this time.

Then we saw them.

Johnson was right, they weren't expecting us.

And we weren't expecting them.

The three of us stared.

'Jesus Christ,' said Johnson.

They weren't Turks. They were British infantry from their uniforms. Those that were still wearing them. Normally I could have had a guess at the regiment from their accents. But they weren't saying anything. Just screaming. Mad with thirst. Staggering around half-naked.

Drinking sand, some of them.

I'd seen tragic things in battles, but nothing like this.

I tried to think straight. There were twenty or thirty of them and we were almost out of water. No water in these dunes.

We had to get them back to camp.

I grabbed Otton and Johnson. The three of us scrambled back to the horses, mounted up and headed down the slope towards the crazed Poms.

Closer we got, the more it felt like a dud idea. Some of the Brits saw us. Ran towards us waving weapons. Faces like you see in an abattoir.

They weren't going to be led anywhere.

I glanced at Otton and Johnson. Otton was rigid with terror. Johnson, who I'd never seen show a flicker of fear, was gob-open with it.

'Come on,' I yelled.

I tried to turn Daisy back up the slope. Before I could, the wind smashed into us and the darkness of swirling sand was on us again.

Daisy staggered but stayed on her feet. I slid off and got her head wrapped again, then mine. I waved to the others to do the same.

We remounted and set off. Daisy and me in front. Me holding Otton's reins behind my back. Otton doing the same with Johnson's.

Single file, small steps, blind.

I tried not to think about the poor blighters we'd just seen. But I couldn't help it. Without Daisy and the other walers, we'd be drinking sand too.

And what if they'd been Turks in that state?

Would we have irrigated the desert with them?

Daisy led us back to camp.

The storm stayed with us the whole way so we just had to trust her.

She didn't let us down.

When we got there the wind was thrashing through the camp. Place was full of rearing horses and flapping tents and yelling officers, so nobody saw us sneak back in.

The three of us looked at each other.

We knew it was a miracle we'd made it.

'Thanks,' I said to Daisy.

Otton thanked her too.

So did Johnson.

'Sorry for what I said,' he muttered. 'About you being ugly.'

Daisy snorted and gave him a look.

Bosworth came over, bent against the wind, his hat tied on with rope.

'Where have you idiots been?' he yelled. 'The tent blew away half an hour ago.'

'Just popped up to Cairo,' said Otton. 'Tea and scones with some nurses.'

Later that afternoon, an even bigger miracle.

A Brit search party, which had been out after their lost troop for two days, found three of their blokes still alive.

Felt like a huge miracle when we heard. But as it turned out, it wasn't.

Not for them or us.

15

'What's going on?' I said to Otton next morning.

Brits were camped next to us. You could see their tents from our horse lines. Three of their blokes were blindfolded and tied to posts.

'Ones they brought in yesterday,' said Otton. 'Gunna cop it.'

I stared.

'Court-martialled for cowardice in the face of the enemy,' said Otton. 'Instead of marching into battle, they went in the opposite direction.'

'That's bull,' I said. 'They were lost in the sand-storm. Couldn't have found the battle with guide dogs.'

Over in the Brit camp, an officer yelled an order. Six infantrymen raised their rifles and took aim.

A firing squad.

That wasn't on.

Nobody would shoot those blokes if they'd seen what the poor blighters went through out there.

I took off.

Running was never my claim to fame, but I got across our campground in double time. Through the wire. Leaping over pommy tent ropes. Throwing myself towards the Brit officer.

Flatten him first, I thought. Explain after.

Before I could get to him, somebody flattened me.

Otton, tackling from behind.

As we hit the dirt, the officer yelled another order. The squad fired. The blokes at the poles went limp.

'You stupid bastard,' I yelled at the Brit officer, struggling up and throwing myself at him. 'They couldn't help it.'

The Brit officer pulled his pistol on me.

I slapped it away. Grabbed him and shook him.

'They were lost,' I yelled.

'Leave it,' hissed Otton, tackling me again.

I wasn't leaving it. I yelled more things at the Brit officer till Otton clamped his hand over my mouth. I tried to struggle free, but Otton hung on to me till the military police arrived and smashed my face into the dirt for a bit, then dragged us both away.

The lock-up was an old stone house in a local village.

I lay on the floor for a while, waiting for my head to stop hurting. Then I opened my eyes.

Otton was sitting against the wall.

'You shouldn't be here,' I mumbled. 'You didn't do anything.'

Otton shrugged.

'Victim of circumstances,' he said.

There was a clatter as the cell door opened. The lock-up sergeant burst in, yelling at us to stand to attention.

We did, slowly.

An Australian major came in and looked us both up and down like we were something in his garden that needed spraying.

'What the blazes?' he demanded.

'It was a misunderstanding, sir,' said Otton.

'No,' barked the major. 'Assaulting an officer is not a misunderstanding. It's an offence that carries a penalty of twelve months hard labour.'

'Those pommy blokes were innocent,' I said. 'That was murder.'

'Listen to me,' growled the major. 'You're out of your depth, son. The Brits shoot their deserters, we don't. So that's a powder keg between us and them for starters. Without you mouthing off about murder.'

'I know what I saw,' I said.

'What you saw doesn't matter, trooper,' said the major. 'Here's what you're going to see. In the morning you're going to see a court-martial. Which will sentence you both to twelve months in a military prison. And when you finally get home, in disgrace, you'll spend the rest of your life seeing the faces of folks who know you're a snivelling cowardly termite who white-anted our war effort.'

'Permission to display a relevant artefact, sir,' said Otton.

The major turned to him angrily.

'It had better be extremely relevant,' he snapped.

'It is, sir,' said Otton.

The lock-up sergeant was sent over to the camp and came back with Daisy's saddlebags.

Otton took out my special bayonet. Held it out to the major. The red glow of the major's cigarette gleamed off each of the jagged teeth.

'This belongs to Trooper Ballantyne, sir,' said Otton. 'Thought you should see it. On account of how you might want to reassess him, sir. On account of how a snivelling cowardly termite probably wouldn't have a superbly engineered killing device such as this.'

The major was silent for a long time.

He stubbed his cigarette out.

'I was wrong when I said twelve months hard labour,' he murmured. 'I didn't know we would also be charging you with possession of an illegal and criminal weapon, for which you will both receive an extra six months.'

He glanced at the lock-up sergeant, nodded towards the bayonet, and walked out.

The lock-up sergeant took the bayonet from Otton, walked to the doorway and paused.

'What you tried to do for them poor Poms,' he said to me, 'I take my hat off to you for that.'

He held up the bayonet.

'But this, you mongrel. For this you deserve everything you're gunna get.'

16

Otton slept that night, I didn't know how.

Sick of the sound of me saying sorry to him, probably.

I sat on the floor of the cell, trying to write a letter to Joan in my head.

Gave up. What was the point?

Tried to sleep. Couldn't.

But being awake didn't stop me having a nightmare.

Not about hard labour. I'd done hard labour all my life. Not even about the sneers on the faces of the folks back home. Sneers only hurt you if you go back home.

My nightmare was about Daisy.

She'd have to stay behind when I was taken away.

Some officer who could spot a top horse would grab her for himself. Have a first ride on her.

Get thrown off, which is what she did to everyone who wasn't me.

Others would try. Same result.

Unrideable horse, they'd say.

Dangerous creature.

The army didn't have feed, or space, for a dangerous creature.

The court-martial next morning wasn't like I'd expected.

No lawyers, no military police, no handcuffs. Just a tent with the sides rolled up and the major sitting at a table.

'At ease,' he said.

Me and Otton tried to stand at ease. But I could see from the major's face we didn't have much reason to.

The major spent a few minutes reading papers in a folder.

Then he gave me a long hard look.

'Trooper Ballantyne,' he said. 'Before we go to the trouble and expense of a full court-martial, I want to give you a choice.'

He paused.

I wasn't sure if I should say anything.

I didn't.

'Your choice is this,' said the major. 'Eighteen months in the military prison in Cairo. Where you will be starved, beaten and worked to within a worm's whisker of your life.'

He paused again. I had a wild thought.

Run for it.

Grab Otton and Daisy.

Ride off into the desert.

I glanced towards the horse lines. And saw I'd been wrong about no military police.

A couple of them, the jacks who'd jumped on my head, were sitting in an armoured car, watching us, rifles on their laps.

'Or,' said the major, 'you can spend the next eighteen months using your special abilities.'

I stared at him.

Special abilities? That could only mean one thing.

Water.

I jumped in too quick. Dad would have gone at me with a bucket.

'I'll do it,' I said.

The major frowned. He was probably wishing he had a bucket himself.

'On two conditions,' I said.

The major gave me a look that said I was lucky to have the use of my head, forget conditions.

'You don't even know what I'm offering,' he said.

'I don't care,' I said. 'As long as I can do it with my horse.' I glanced at Otton. 'And my mate.'

The major sighed.

'Oh, how I wish,' he murmured, 'the army still allowed flogging.'

He closed the folder.

'You start tomorrow,' he said.

17

'We're not plumbers,' I said bitterly. 'We're troopers.'

Otton groaned and pushed up his welding mask.

'Will you stop saying that,' he said. 'You've been saying that for a month. If I have to spend the next fifteen months listening to you whingeing I will weld you inside this infernal thing and that's a non-revisable promise.'

I pushed my own welding mask up and squinted at the pipeline snaking across the desert. And at the Egyptian workers toiling on it, supervised by engineers from about six countries.

'All I'm saying,' I said, 'is these blokes don't need our help. The blokes on the front line are the ones who need our help.'

Otton dropped his welding gear, grabbed the front of my shirt and dragged me over to where

Daisy and his horse were standing in the shade of a pile of pipe sections.

'Tell him,' Otton said to Daisy. 'Tell him how this work is just as important as fighting the Turks. Tell him how if the army wasn't putting this pipeline in, our blokes wouldn't be fighting any Turks on account of they wouldn't have any water.'

Daisy gave me a look.

I knew she didn't get all the nuances of Otton's argument, but I also knew she was a big fan of the pipeline. Fresh water every day, no drilling.

'All I'm saying,' I said, 'is that back home the volunteers have dried up, the chooks are naked from so many white feathers being chucked around, and the government's talking about forcing blokes into the army. And here we are, two able-bodied fighting men, turning eighteen and legal in a few months, stuck here being plumbers.'

Otton sighed.

'Allow me to paraphrase,' he said. 'What you're saying is, you got us into this mess, you take full responsibility for your nong behaviour, and you're terrified the war will end and leave you with an unavenged father and a plumber's medal.'

'Yes,' I said quietly.

I hadn't mentioned Dad or Joan for weeks. But Otton knew they were eating at my guts.

'Right-o,' said Otton. 'Why don't we make a deal. A bilateral treaty. You pull your head in and don't do anything stupid that ends us in the Cairo clink. And I'll use my talents to get us time off for good behaviour. So we can get back to the front line.'

I thought about this.

'You're on,' I said. 'Thanks.'

'So,' said Otton. 'That's a lot of *sang-froid* and patience from you, and a lot of ingratiating and bum-licking from me.'

Daisy helped me keep my side of the bargain.

As the months went by, and our blokes fought their way into Palestine, we were behind them with the pipeline all the way.

I kept my mind active, thinking about what I'd do when I got back into battle.

At night, in my swag, I'd stare up at the stars, waiting for my brain to follow my tuckered-out body into sleep.

Daisy would lie down next to me sometimes, on the really cold nights.

I'd feel her heart next to my ear, slow and steady.

The most loyal heart in the world it felt like.

Otton kept his half of the deal.

Took him a year, but he did it.

Friday and Saturday nights he sang in our Officers' Mess. Other officers from fighting units were there sometimes, and Otton ended up mates with a few.

Finally, he got some strings pulled.

'Big battle coming up,' said Otton excitedly. 'All the Light Horse for yonks around are in it. Us included.'

I couldn't believe it.

I didn't hug blokes as a rule, but I hugged Otton.

'We're back with our troop tomorrow,' he said. 'Back in the thick of it.'

My brain was spinning.

'Where's the battle?' I said.

Otton frowned.

'Place in Palestine I haven't heard of,' he said. 'Beersheba.'

18

It was grand to see the old faces.

They were chuffed to see us, Bosworth and Lesney specially.

'What kept you?' said Bosworth. 'Afternoon tea in Cairo again? Did the nurses make you wash the dishes?'

Lots of chiacking, but I could see how tense the blokes were underneath. They knew this was a big one. Most important battle we'd fronted up for. Do-or-die effort.

Daisy must have known it was serious too. Muster and decampment in the dark. Usual long hot ride to the battle spot. Got there dusty and tired. Not a complaint from her.

On the battlefield we saw straight off this was a different class of stoush.

Our infantry had been going at it for hours.

Big Turkish defence lines. Miles of trenches. Infantry stopped whingeing for a change. Almost broke through.

But they didn't. Poor blighters were getting mowed down.

Then the order came.

We'd waited two years for this.

Gallop at the Turks. Break through the mongrels on horseback. No horse-holding here. We were all in it. Well and truly in it.

Charge!

Galloping hard across four miles of open desert. Hundreds of us but we were soon spread.

Couldn't even see the Turkish trenches through our own dust. But they could see us. Machine-guns, artillery, they let us know they could see us.

Otton was next to me. His usual style of riding. Hang on and pray. Harder for him today because we had bayonets in hand.

Regulation ones, but they'd do the job.

I should have been yelling with excitement like the other blokes. This was my chance. Give the mongrels a big serve for Dad. Rack up some corpses to impress Joan's folks. I should have been happier than a wagtail in a wheat field.

But I wasn't.

I kept seeing the face of the Turk I'd let go.

Would it be the same this time? Would I pike out at the last minute?

Horses started going down. Men screaming. Horses screaming.

Suddenly I could see the trenches.

Blokes were diving off their horses on to the Turks. Vicious fighting. Chaotic.

Johnson in the thick of it.

I went in after them. And saw what the Turks were doing. Targetting the horses. Bayonets into their bellies as they reached the trenches. Bullets into their throats.

The horses without riders were trying to get away.

Machine-gunned. Blown to pieces.

Two Turks in weird camouflage jackets rose up out of a trench, guns aimed at Daisy.

No time to turn her away.

I swung my rifle round from my back, clamped it tight against my side and pulled the trigger. Trained for this, but it still nearly kicked me out of the saddle.

One of the Turks went down. So did my rifle, out of my grasp.

Daisy didn't stop. Straight at the other Turk.

I gave him my bayonet.

In deep.

Daisy leaped over the trench.

I took her reins in both hands. Urged her on and we flew. Soared over trench after trench. She never faltered, never wavered.

Otton was doing the same I hoped. But I couldn't see him.

Next thing, we were behind the trenches.

In the town. It was almost deserted. Few Turks running. Couple of our scouts yelled at me.

'Stop the mongrels duffing the wells.'

I saw what they meant.

Turks in the town square were trying to blow up the wells. So we'd have no water after the battle. Pipeline was hours away. We'd never have made it.

The scouts dealt with the Turks. I dealt with the explosives. When you knew wells, you knew where the charges'd be.

They did a top job, those scouts. I was down deep, dragging detonator wire out of the rock crevices. A desperate Turk tried to lob a grenade down on to me. Scouts showed him the error of his ways.

I saw his body by the well-mouth when I came up. And the crater the grenade had made over the other side of the square.

Then I saw that Daisy was bleeding.

She was standing where I'd left her, trembling.

Her chest and flanks were red.

At first I thought she'd copped shrapnel from the grenade. But I looked closer and it wasn't that. It was bayonet wounds. Turks must have got her as we jumped the trenches.

I grabbed water from one of the wells and tore my shirt into pieces and wiped away the blood, gentle as I could.

They'd got her five times. But not deep. She must have been flying too fast.

'Easy, mate,' I said. 'Have to get these clean. Don't want you festering up.'

She understood. Calm and balanced.

Me and Dad knew what to do when a horse got cut. Boil up sprigs of lemon myrtle and dab it on. But you couldn't get lemon myrtle in Palestine, so I mixed disinfectant and chlorine tablets from my first-aid kit and used that.

'We'll have you right in no time,' I said to Daisy. 'Rested up and fit as a fence post.'

I didn't tell her how important that was. Or just how much depended on it.

In the distance I could hear gunshots out on the battlefield, even though the battle had been over for a while. No place for wounded horses in an army on the move.

'Trooper, attenshun,' roared a voice.

I turned. Commotion behind me. Our blokes leading their horses to canvas troughs being set up near the wells. Everyone desperate for water.

A sergeant yelling at me.

Behind him, a captain.

I stood to attention. Praying I'd patched Daisy up sufficient so they wouldn't see how wounded she was.

'Is this the one?' demanded the captain.

'Yes, sir,' yelled the sergeant.

I stood rigid, ready to hurl myself at them if they tried to shoot Daisy.

'Good work, trooper,' said the captain.

I blinked, confused.

'The Beersheba wells are of immense strategic significance,' said the captain. 'Superb initiative, that response of yours.'

I didn't know what to say.

Strategic significance? Superb initiative?

Where was Otton when you needed him.

'Ballantyne's our water monkey, sir,' said a voice. 'He's got a nose for it.'

It was Bosworth.

Lesney with him.

'Very well done,' said the captain to me. 'I'll be recommending you for a commendation.'

He saluted, the sergeant saluted, I saluted,

Bosworth and Lesney saluted, and then the officers were gone.

'Jeez,' said Bosworth. 'You're getting a medal.'

I was chuffed of course, but there were more important things.

'Rather have ointment for Daisy,' I said, checking to see how her bleeding was going.

It wasn't so bad now. I stroked her head. I could see she agreed about the ointment.

'Wait on,' I said, remembering. 'Otton's got ointment. For his feet.'

Bosworth and Lesney didn't say anything.

'Where is Otton?' I said.

Bosworth and Lesney still didn't say anything.

They didn't need to.

Their faces said it for them.

19

We found Otton on the plain we'd charged across. About a hundred yards from the trenches. Lying under his horse.

Both of them taken by the machine-guns.

I sank to my knees next to them.

When I opened my eyes, I saw it wasn't just a battlefield any more. It was a cemetery. Dozens of graves being dug.

Blokes who'd tried to do their bit.

We dug a grave for Otton. I'd have buried his horse as well, but the ground was too hard and rocky. We didn't have the right gear. We barely managed to get down deep enough for Otton's skinny body.

Gently we lowered him into the earth. I put his songbook onto his chest. The chaplain appeared, said a few words and moved on.

Then we covered our Australian mate with Palestinian soil. We scratched his name on to the stock of his rifle, stuck it into the ground as a grave marker, and tied his emu feather hat to it.

Me and Bosworth and Lesney stood, heads bowed, and said our silent words.

We stood for a long time.

Late that night, I did something else.

Didn't tell anyone about it on account of they probably wouldn't understand and they might very likely take it the wrong way.

I crept out of camp with Daisy.

Back to the Turkish lines. Found the spot where me and her first hit their trenches.

There were plenty of Turkish bodies still unburied. After a lot of hunting I found my rifle. Near to it was my bayonet, deep in the body of a bloke wearing a camouflage jacket. Next to him was another bloke, same jacket, bullet hole in the guts.

My bullet hole, I reckoned.

I lifted the two Turkish blokes onto Daisy's back. She bowed her head and we walked out into the open desert. I found a spot and dug two graves.

As gently as I could I lifted the Turkish blokes down and buried them.

I stood by the graves. Wasn't sure what to say. Stayed there anyway.

After a while, I felt Daisy's head on my shoulder.

Truth was I didn't know those blokes at all. But thinking about them made me think about Dad, and soon my whole body was shaking with tears.

20

In war you never knew what was up ahead. Sure as tinned meat I didn't.

Starting with Joan's parcel.

It arrived six months after Beersheba.

I'd had a pretty low Christmas on account of Otton. Pretty low start to 1918, too. Bosworth and Lesney were posted further north. After Beersheba they'd wanted to go back into the water deployment unit with me, but the brass made them stay with the fighting.

Daisy came with me of course. The army had abandoned the pipeline and we were foraging water on the run as we pushed the Turks back towards their joint.

I saw Johnson one night in April, heading off on one of his solo hunting trips. He told me how a really crook thing had happened the week before.

Bosworth and Lesney had been killed by snipers. One careless campfire, six blokes gone.

'Tonight's for them,' said Johnson.

His face and his bayonet both had boot polish on them. But I could still see the gleaming teeth. His and the bayonet's.

I didn't go. My place was with Daisy.

I was knocked hard by the news. Very sad I'd missed both their funerals. So me and Daisy had our own. Just a few words into an old well and a cup of water each in their memory.

Few weeks later Joan's parcel arrived. Day after my nineteenth birthday.

Nearly three years I'd been waiting to hear from her and now, out of the blue, a hefty parcel tied up with eight miles of string.

Couldn't hardly get it open, I was so excited.

Finally did, and everything fell out. Two pairs of socks. Four tins of meat. Sugar lumps for Daisy. Cough lozenges for me. Half a page from the local paper with a mention of my medal. More socks.

And a letter.

Dear Francis,

I read in the newspaper recently about your medal. Congratulations on your wonderful contribution to our war effort.

Last year I also read about the loss of your father. Please accept my condolences. My father was killed in France, so I know how you feel.

They were both men of great bravery and patriotism, and so I wish to apologise for the white feather my mother and her friends sent to your father. At the time they thought it was the right thing to do, but now they know it was wrong.

Please accept this apology, dear Francis.

I must also ask you something very difficult. I must ask that you stop writing to me. I am engaged to be married, and at the request of my fiancé I have been disposing of your letters unread for the last year.

Yours warmly, but in future sincerely,

Joan.

PS Happy birthday. Say g'day to Daisy for me.

I disposed of her letter too.

But not unread.

I read it about a hundred times. Then I went out into the desert and built a small fire, inside a billy so no enemy sniper would spot the burning letter and get me through the heart like it had.

I stared at the flames, and then the embers, and then the cold ashes.

After a long time, I realised Daisy was looking at me. Sympathy on her face.

Some wouldn't have reckoned that was possible, but I saw it. Daisy knew about heartache.

'Thanks,' I said to her. 'A bloke with half a brain would probably have spotted this coming.'

Daisy didn't comment.

Just chewed a sugar lump.

'Some of us creatures might think we're smarter than other creatures,' I said to her. 'But we're not. We get an idea in our head and we hang on to it even when a six-year-old could tell us it's a dopey one.'

Daisy gently blew sugary air into my face.

I wasn't just talking about me and Joan.

Otton had tried to explain to me how this war started. I didn't grasp all the details, but when he talked about the squabbling between France and Germany and England and Russia and Serbia and the rest, I could see it wasn't real smart.

Didn't matter now.

Blokes were doing their bit. Giving their all.

We had a job to do.

I emptied the billy, wiped it out, and we headed back to camp for a feed and a sleep.

'It's just you and me now,' I said to Daisy.

21

The Turks had got Dad. They'd got Otton and Bosworth and Lesney.

But they weren't getting Daisy.

Was I certain about that?

Oath I was.

If only I'd known.

When we were on the move at night, I covered Daisy's white bits with black boot polish. Knew she wouldn't like it, so I put some on my face as well.

'They'll need good eyesight now, those snipers,' I said to her. 'Inordinate good eyesight.'

Daisy gave me a look.

I knew what she was probably thinking. Me and her hadn't had a bath for weeks. Snipers could probably locate us blindfolded.

At least the mongrels had plenty of choice for targets. We were a big mob now.

Not just the Light Horse. Mounted troops from Britain, Canada, all over. Biggest horseback army since Genghis Khan, someone said.

Dunno what Genghis did for water, but as we pushed the Turks and their Hun friends north towards Damascus, we had to work hard for ours.

I wouldn't have reckoned it, but water was harder to find in the desert in winter than in summer. Everything froze up at night. Which is why me and Daisy took the risks we did.

Blokes and horses needed water just as much in winter as they did when it was scorching. More if they were sniffling and crook, and hot soup was the only thing keeping the influenza off them.

Me and Daisy were on the move the whole time. Ahead of the troops, behind the troops, off to one side, off to the other side. Unclogging wells, melting ice in caves, stopping drill rigs from rusting with sand rubs and camel fat.

We kept our heads down.

Enemy knew our whole advance would be cactus if we didn't have water. So their snipers went at us night and day. Water deployment units copped more airborne lead than the average fairground duck.

Daisy didn't like it, being shot at. As we advanced, if we came across a deserted sniper hideout, she'd give it a good hosing.

Not a single enemy bullet touched me or her.

I wished Otton could have been there to see it. He was a cheery bugger most of the time, and he'd have enjoyed our good fortune.

Probably have called it mellifluous or some such.

They were good months for me and Daisy. We were cold, hungry, weary and scared, but we were together and we kept each other going.

And at night, when we kipped together for warmth, both of us were always grateful for what that warmth told us. That we each had someone we cared about left in the world.

Though Daisy had someone else as well.

I thought about Daisy's daughter a fair bit. How we'd get her back after the war and have her live with us.

Then one night, when me and Daisy were camped out in the desert on a water recce by ourselves, her daughter turned up in a dream.

Me and Daisy are riding across central New South Wales in the dark. The warm night air is fragrant with eucalypt and lemon myrtle and other smells you didn't get in Palestine, like roast pork.

Dawn starts to come up.

We arrive at a paddock. The lush grass is wet with

dew and scattered with mist. Fingers of sunlight stroke their way across the grass. Just like when I used to get up early to help Mum with the milking.

I'm standing next to Daisy and suddenly she starts to tremble.

Out of the golden mist comes a beautiful young horse. For a sec I think she's Daisy. She's not, she's smaller, but she's got Daisy's white flashes and lop-sided body, exact.

Daisy runs to her.

They stand together for a moment. Then gallop, side by side, mist streaming off them, joyful.

Me as well, running with them.

Joyful.

I woke up.

Normally, next to me on the desert hillside, Daisy's dark ribs would have been slowly rising and falling. Normally I would have felt the warmth of her.

But she wasn't there.

I sat up, panicked.

And saw her. Up on the ridgeline. Silhouetted against what Otton used to call the vault of stars.

She wasn't galloping, she was standing rock-still.

Head up, staring at the horizon.

In the distance was the rumble of artillery fire.

Or thunder. Or maybe it was just my heart beating.

I whistled to Daisy.

She wheeled round, stared at me for a few moments, as if she wasn't sure who I was, then thundered down the hillside towards me.

I braced myself for a warm wet nuzzle.

Instead she stopped a few paces away, white breath cascading from her nostrils, chest gleaming with sweat.

Her eyes somewhere else.

I waited a while, then started to gently rub her down with my blanket.

'Don't worry,' I said. 'We'll get her back.'

Slowly Daisy relaxed.

Her eyes softened. Went big and sad.

She put her head on my shoulder.

I gave her the last of Joan's sugar lumps. My hand was trembling. Daisy was too.

Next morning, though, she was fine.

Could all have been a dream if my blanket hadn't still been damp with her sweat and I hadn't still been shivering from trying to sleep under it.

I stroked Daisy's neck while she was having breakfast.

'I mean it,' I said. 'We'll get her back.'

The other thing that kept us going was we knew the Turks and Huns were finished. Just a matter of time.

And exactly a year to the day after we charged them at Beersheba, they packed it in.

Mass surrenderings all over the place.

Huns in France included.

Jeez, we celebrated. Big cup of tea, real tea. Oats for Daisy, real oats from the officers' mess.

'Good on you, cobber,' I said to her. 'We made it.'

The war was over.

But not for me and Daisy.

22

It was a chook-house of a way to end a war.

The fighting was over, but our military duties weren't. We were turned into sort of police.

The local folk had gone a bit hysterical after having foreigners fighting a war in their country for four years. I didn't blame them, but the brass reckoned they needed a bit of supervising.

So we did. Me and Daisy didn't mind. At least nobody was shooting.

Not yet.

Back in camp, between shifts, we made plans for the future.

'When we get back home there'll be parades,' I said to Daisy. 'Big one down the main street of Sydney, probably. And down the main street of our town, but we won't bother with that one.'

Daisy understood. One parade's enough.

Start getting too full of yourself with more than one.

'We'll get ourselves a piece of land,' I said to her. 'Word is, government'll give us soldiers a loan so we can pay some acres off. Wait till you see what it's like over Gulgong way. Near Ulan Drip. Water there, permanent.'

Daisy wouldn't have understood every word, but she could see how excited I was, so she knew how good it would be.

'Then,' I said, 'we'll find your daughter. I know which property out west she's on, and I'll have a whack of army pay. If the farmer doesn't want to sell her, I'll just offer him more.'

Daisy looked at me.

'And then,' I said, 'it'll be the three of us on our place, together. All right, four if I can find a sheila.'

Daisy licked my ear.

It was her way of telling me to go for it.

One morning I stuck my head out of the tent and saw the remount quartermaster over by the horse lines. Talking with a bloke in a strange-looking uniform.

I went over.

The bloke, I saw as I got closer, was an officer

from some other army. Indian, it looked like.

He was having a close squiz at our horses.

'Hmmm,' he was saying. 'Damage on this one too. Barbed-wire scars, I'd say.'

At first I thought he was a vet. Brought in by the brass to give our horses a bit of medical attention before the long voyage home. Which was what they deserved.

'I'm puzzled,' the Indian officer said. 'Isn't it standard practise on the battlefield to dispose of wounded horses?'

The quartermaster nodded.

'The bad ones,' he said. 'But our walers are tough. Few scratches don't bother 'em.'

The Indian officer frowned.

'I'm afraid we can only take the unmarked ones,' he said.

I wasn't sure I'd heard right.

Take? Take where? And why would a vet only be interested in the ones that hadn't been in strife?

'What if,' said the quartermaster, 'we chuck in the damaged ones free of charge? You only buy the clean ones.'

I couldn't believe what I was hearing.

Free of charge? Buy?

'What's going on?' I said.

There were other troopers with me now, muttering, concerned.

The quartermaster hadn't seen us come over. For a second he looked at us nervously, then glared at us.

'Back to your tents,' he roared. 'That's an order.'

None of us moved.

I could see Daisy on the line, watching us.

'What the hell is going on?' said a trooper near me, slowly and clearly so even the quartermaster's fat ears could get the gist.

'This prawn,' said another trooper, pointing to the Indian officer. 'What's he up to?'

The Indian officer looked very annoyed.

'The army of India is doing the Australian army a favour,' he said to the quartermaster. 'It's bad enough you're trying to sell us damaged stock. We will not put up with abuse as well.'

Sell?

I couldn't believe it. Our loyal horses, who'd worked their guts out for their country, were being sold off to work their guts out again in some other bloke's war.

Not on.

'The damaged ones stay,' said the Indian officer. 'My orders are to take only healthy stock.'

I had a selfish thought.

At least they wouldn't want Daisy, not with her bayonet wounds.

But for the others, not on.

I went to grab a fistful of the Indian officer's jacket. One of the other troopers beat me to it.

'You touch any of those horses,' the trooper said to the Indian officer, 'and you'll be copping more than abuse. Your wallet stays in your pocket, Mahatma, you got that?'

Me and the other troopers agreed with him.

Loudly.

The quartermaster blew a whistle.

Next thing I was on the ground, face in the dust. I felt handcuffs on my wrists. Two military police dragged me to my feet.

I couldn't believe it.

Military police were swarming all over the place, armed and organised. We'd never had mobs of jacks like this in our camp. They must have been brought in specially. On account of the brass knowing how we'd feel, having our horses sold behind our backs.

Some of the other blokes were handcuffed too. The rest were standing back, looking dazed.

'You can't do this, you mongrel,' I said to the quartermaster.

He sighed. For a long moment I thought he was going to agree.

But when he replied, he didn't look any of us in the eye.

'Orders from the top,' the quartermaster said. 'These aren't horses any more. They're surplus military equipment.'

I tried to get to him. Shake him till he came to his senses. But the jacks dragged me in the opposite direction.

Daisy was still watching us.

At least she was safe.

23

After I cooled down in the lock-up, I worked out what to do.

'How long?' I said to the lock-up sergeant.

'Forty-eight hours,' he said. 'You're lucky. If we were still at war, with your record, you'd be doing serious time.'

'No,' I said, 'I mean how long till the horses get sent to India?'

The lock-up sergeant shrugged.

'They'll be taking 'em by train to the coast,' he said. 'Putting 'em on a boat. Train track got blown up, so they'll have to repair that first.'

Good.

Enough time to write to General Chauvel and General Allenby. Remind them how the Turks and Huns'd be dancing on our graves if it wasn't for our walers. Point out that a horse can be a war hero just as much as a bloke. If heroic generals get to go home after the war for a rest and a pat on the back, so should heroic horses.

I wrote all that out.

'Can you send these for me?' I said to the lock-up sergeant.

The sergeant looked at the sheets of toilet paper I handed him. Shook his head.

'Troopers don't write to generals,' he said.

Soon as I got out of the lock-up, I checked on Daisy.

She was tethered on the line, feed bag full and plenty of water. So were all the other horses, even the sold ones. The lock-up sergeant must have been right about the delay for train-track repairs.

'Good to see they're looking after you,' I said to Daisy. 'Even if you are damaged goods.'

I tickled her under the chin while I said it, so she'd know I was joshing.

She looked at me and her big eyes were sadder than I'd ever seen them.

'Don't worry,' I said. 'There's still hope for your mates. I've put in for a face-to-face with the colonel.'

In the army anyone could put in for a face-to-face with their commanding officer.

But the rules said the commanding officer could pike out and offload the meeting to a lower-ranking officer. And the lower-ranking officer could shunt the meeting to an even lower-ranking officer. And so on.

I got a troop sergeant.

'At ease,' said the troop sergeant, leaning back and putting his feet on a table in a bar in the local town. 'Smoke if you want to.'

I didn't want to.

'It's like this,' I said. 'You don't sell blokes to other armies. Why are horses different?'

The sergeant rolled his eyes.

'They're horses,' he said.

'They're our mates,' I said.

'The Australian army is not a bleedin' friendship society,' said the sergeant. 'We've got tens of thousands of enlisted men to get home. Blokes are more important than horses, end of story.'

'What about Sandy?' I said. 'That horse who belonged to that Aussie Major General who copped it at Gallipoli. They're sending him home.'

'Yeah,' said the sergeant. 'And the whole catastrophe's gunna take six months. Quarantine in England. Quarantine in Sydney. Medical tests all over the place. Costing a heap. Army reckons never again.'

'So our mates get dumped in India,' I said angrily, 'just cause it's too much trouble to bring 'em home.'

'They're the lucky ones,' he said.

We stared at each other.

I felt something go tight in my guts.

'What d'you mean?' I said. 'What'll happen to the ones the Indian army doesn't want?'

The sergeant didn't say anything. Just sighed. Took a pull on his beer. Lit another cigarette.

'What'll happen to them?' I said.

'Why don't you have a beer,' said the sergeant. 'Have lots of beers. That's what all your mates are doing.'

I looked around the bar. Full of troopers. Drinking hard.

Looking gutted.

'I'm going back to camp,' I said.

'I wouldn't,' said the sergeant.

Camp was chaos.

Troopers running all over the shop, dragging their horses. Like they were trying to get away from something, but they didn't know where to go.

Officers walking fast, wiping their eyes.

I asked a couple of blokes what was happening.

They didn't even hear me.

These were blokes whose horses hadn't been sold. They should have been feeling relieved. Didn't look like they were.

'It's all right, mate,' I said when I got to where Daisy was tethered.

Why was she trembling? She knew she could trust me. I'd brought her over, I'd take her back.

She gazed at me and I saw a look in her eyes. One I hadn't seen before. I didn't know exactly what it was, but I could see she knew something I didn't.

'What?' I said.

Of course she couldn't tell me, so I went to investigate.

A fenced-in enclosure. Beyond the far side of the camp. Behind a grove of date palms. Rough job. Six-foot plank fence that looked like it had been knocked together in a hurry.

I peered over.

And saw why our blokes were so worked up.

Twenty or so of our horses, tethered to posts. Heads down. Feet moving anxiously. No manes. No tails. Someone had cut their manes and tails off.

I didn't understand.

Troops up the other end of the pen, not our blokes, infantry by the look. Shoulders slumped. Standing around something that shouldn't have been there.

A machine-gun.

Gunner sitting in position. Threw his cigarette away. Took aim at the horses.

I stared. Tried to yell.

My throat was frozen.

I dropped. Lay in the dust and put my hands over my ears. But I still heard it.

I heard it all.

24

'They will not all be shot,' yelled the remount quartermaster, standing at his desk. 'The unsold horses will not all be shot.'

We didn't believe him. We could all hear the machine-gun in the distance.

There must have been a hundred blokes in that tent. All of us in shock. All of us ropeable and letting him know.

'Shooting horses is a last resort,' the quartermaster yelled over the din. 'You have my word.'

How could we trust him? How could we trust an army that would machine-gun its own horses?

It was down to us now.

Blokes pleaded. Threatened. Tried bribery.

Me included.

No good.

Military police pushed us back from the desk.

The remount quartermaster slumped in his office chair and put his head in his hands. A troop sergeant stood next to him and yelled at us.

'None of us like this,' he shouted.

He didn't look too unhappy to me. I remembered this sergeant. Before Beersheba he'd reckoned the army should get rid of all its horses and replace them with tanks.

'Orders have been issued,' yelled the sergeant. 'I quote. Military property is the property of the military.'

We didn't hear any more of what he said. He was drowned out by a hundred furious voices.

The remount quartermaster stood up and raised his hands pleadingly. We quietened down. Just in case he had something half-decent to say.

'The British army have agreed to take some of the damaged mounts,' said the quartermaster. 'So have local horse dealers.'

'How many will they take?' somebody yelled.

'How many won't they take?' shouted somebody else.

Every bloke there was wondering the same thing. There were a lot of Light Horse camps in Palestine. A lot of Aussie horses.

How many of them had battle scars?

Five thousand?

Ten?

'How many *won't* they take?' repeated the angry voices.

The quartermaster didn't reply. He stared down at his desk. We could see tears in his eyes.

Suddenly there was a disturbance up the back. Somebody shouting in a foreign accent. A bloke in a blood-smeared smock, a local.

He squeezed through the crowd. Looked around. Decided the military police were the ones to talk to.

'I'm coming for the hides,' he said.

The military police looked confused. The bloke waved a piece of paper at them.

'Hides,' he said. 'Selling from army.'

I grabbed the paper. It was a bill of sale, an official army form. One hundred hides, one hundred tails and manes, four hundred hooves.

Another trooper snatched the paper. I let him take it.

I was numb.

At least this answered the question I'd been asking myself. Why were the army destroying their own property?

They weren't destroying it.

They were selling it off.

Bit by bit.

Well, no way was Daisy ending up in pieces.

The tent was a pig fight. Troopers snatching the paper from hand to hand, reading it, staring at it, horrified. Others trying to get their hands on the local trader. The jacks stopping them.

I backed away.

Yelling and rioting wasn't going to save Daisy.

Stay calm.

Balanced.

Think this through.

25

Posh hotels in Palestine didn't get many horses in them. Not from the looks Daisy and me were getting.

I didn't care.

Daisy didn't either. She stood there, head high.

'You're right, she's got a few nicks,' I said to the Indian purchasing officer. 'But deep down she's a gem. And don't be put off by her shape. She's a champ.'

The officer gave me a dark look. Apologised to the other two officers he was having tea with. Got up from the table. Led me and Daisy over to the other side of the hotel garden.

'The consignment is complete,' he said.

I didn't need Otton to explain what that meant. It meant they were chokka with our horses.

'You'll want to make room for Daisy,' I said.

'She's something special. Plus you'll get me. No charge for either.'

The officer looked like his cake had gone down the wrong way. I pushed on, trying not to show how desperate I was.

'Three-and-a-half years military experience, both of us,' I said. 'Wells and pipelines. Don't tell me India hasn't got dry bits.'

'This is absurd,' said the officer. 'I'm reporting this to your senior officer.'

'Fair go,' I said, putting my arm round Daisy. 'Give her a break. Please.'

But I could see she wasn't going to get it.

Not in this posh hotel.

A couple of their security blokes were coming towards us, so I got her out of there.

'Eighty quid,' I said to the British despatch sergeant at the railway depot. 'Put her on the train for Blighty and I'll give you eighty quid.'

The sergeant pushed away a couple of other blokes who were trying to get his attention by grabbing his chin-strap. He looked at what I was holding out to him.

'That's not eighty quid,' he said. 'That's a piece of paper with your untidy scrawl on it.'

'It's an IOU,' I said. 'My demob pay will be at least eighty quid. Soon as I'm a civvy I'll come straight to England and give you the cash.'

I didn't tell him how I'd get myself there if I was using all my dough to buy Daisy her life.

I didn't know. But I'd do it.

'Sorry, matey,' said the despatch sergeant. 'I'm a loyal son of England. I only get corrupted by bits of paper with His Majesty's gob on it.'

He turned to the other two blokes, who were waving IOUs at him as well. So were a crowd of blokes behind them.

'Serious customers only,' he said. 'Hundred quid one way, neddie class, standing room only, payment up front, no home-made currency.'

I wasn't the only one without the cash.

The railway depot was swarming with dejected troopers leading their horses back towards camp. We walked past a train packed with English horses happy to be heading home.

'Sorry, mate,' I said to Daisy. 'I thought an IOU would do it. But some of us humans aren't as trusting as you lot.'

I led her away.

Not towards camp. My ideas hadn't dried up yet.

The local horse dealers fell in love with Daisy the moment I showed them the four pounds six shillings, which was every penny I had in the world till I got my demob pay.

'Good home for lovely horse, *effendi*,' they said. 'Much kindness. Much comfort.'

Trouble was, me and Daisy didn't fall in love with the local horse dealers. We didn't even like them. I was very tempted to do to them exactly what they did to their horses.

'Much kindness, much comfort, *effendi*.'

Hanging from the belt of every dealer who said that was a vicious-looking whip and a couple of canes. And every poor nag we saw, in a whole street of dealers' yards, was in a tragic state.

Starved.

Beaten.

Diseased.

I could hardly look at the poor blighters.

Daisy looked at them for a long time, whinnying softly and blowing air at them.

Horses don't cry, everyone knows that, but Daisy came close that day.

I tried to think it through.

Healthy horse like Daisy would be sold quick. So she wouldn't spend much time with these cruel mongrels.

Plus the four pounds six shillings would pay for decent feed while she was here.

If she was lucky.

Then I remembered the working horses we saw the day we got off the boat. Dropping with exhaustion. Beaten where they lay.

Daisy had seen them too.

Which was why she wanted to get closer to the poor wrecked horses in the dealers' yards. To give them a moment of sympathy in their unhappy painful lives.

But she didn't want to be one of them. Not permanent. I could see that for a fact.

'Come on, mate,' I said to her. 'Let's get out of here.'

26

We got out of there all right.

All the way out.

After dark I led Daisy out of camp. She was saddled up and kitted out and loaded with extra food and water. Which technically I was stealing from the army. But as I wasn't going to be around to get my demob pay, it seemed fair.

'Where's your pass?' said the guard at the gate.

I didn't have one so I gave him the four pounds six shillings, which did the trick.

Daisy and me rode into the desert.

South.

I wasn't exactly sure where we were heading. Not long term. When you leave school at eleven, you don't carry much in the way of geography around with you. I had a notion Africa was ahead of us somewhere.

Persia maybe.

Didn't matter. Important thing was we were headed away from the machine-guns. Which, if you were a horse, smashed your legs and punctured your lungs and left you in agony on the ground until some bloke with a pistol strolled over and finished you with a bullet in the head.

'You all right, Daisy?' I said.

I could tell from her easy breathing and relaxed gait as we jogged across the sand in the moonlight that she was.

'Dunno where we're headed,' I said. 'But I'm glad we're going there together.'

Daisy didn't slow down, so she must have felt the same way.

Every so often I glanced over my shoulder to see if we were being followed.

We weren't.

But something was nagging at me.

Was there something I'd forgotten that could be coming after us?

It wasn't behind us, it was ahead of us.

In a shallow gulley. I didn't see it till we'd almost reached it. By then the moon had climbed a smidge and lit up the full horror of them.

Horses and men, on the sand.

I'd seen plenty of death, but I'd never seen the bodies of horses and men treated like these had been.

They were troopers and their walers, doing the same as me and Daisy.

Getting out.

But like me, they'd forgotten about something.

The Bedouin.

I buried the bodies. Couldn't leave them for the jackals. Not that the jackals could have done much worse to them.

Daisy stood patiently, watching.

While I dug, I explained to her about the Bedouin. Desert nomads. Of all the local people, they were the most angry. Felt the desert was theirs. Hated us foreigners coming in and shooting the place up. Wanted to make their point before we left.

'We've got a lot of desert ahead of us,' I said to Daisy. 'Lot of Bedouin ahead of us too. Can't promise we won't bump into them.'

I didn't tell her I thought we probably would.

She watched me drag a mutilated body into a grave.

'What I can promise,' I said softly, 'is I wouldn't let them kill you this way.'

Daisy didn't move.

I couldn't trust my voice to get any more words out, so I patted my rifle. I watched Daisy closely, to see if she understood.

I think she did.

She was looking at me calmly.

Like always, she'd thought it through.

While I finished the burying, Daisy had a nap. Head down, feet apart in the sand, knees locked.

Seeing her sleep standing up always made me smile.

Somehow I managed one now.

As I dug, I got to mulling over all the things I admired about her.

Her kindness. Her patience. How she'd go for fourteen hours across the scorching desert without complaining. Her loyalty. Her bravery. How she could sense danger in the dark.

But not while she was asleep.

Which is how come neither of us spotted them creeping up on us.

27

Not the Bedouin, the military police.

'You're nicked,' said a triumphant voice, and a couple of sides of beef walloped me into the sand.

The jacks had twigged what was going on. Distraught troopers and army property making a break for it.

Deserting, they reckoned it was.

They stuck a bag over Daisy's head and one over mine.

I reached out and found Daisy's neck and gave it a stroke.

'I won't desert you,' I whispered to her.

'That's rich,' said one of the jacks. 'A deserter's still a deserter even when the war's over. We don't shoot you bludgers like the poms do, but you'll grow moss on your north side in jail.'

I was quiet as they took us back to camp.

They probably thought I was a wuss.

I didn't care.

Important thing was, I had a bit of time. They wouldn't be machine-gunning Daisy straight away. I heard the jacks talking about the backlog that had built up. Other camps were sending some of their horses to us.

'Lazy mongrels,' said one of the jacks. 'I mean how much effort is it to pull a trigger?'

'Welcome back,' said the lock-up sergeant as he locked me up.

I was in one of the few brick buildings in the camp, but sounds from the outside still made it through the wall.

Machine-gun sounds mostly.

Every half hour. Right through the day.

I tried to block them out. I tried to block everything out. I couldn't.

I kept thinking of Dad in his trench at Gallipoli. How much he probably hadn't wanted to take his next step.

But he took it.

I banged on the cell door with my fists.

'I need an hour,' I said to the lock-up sergeant.

The sergeant unfolded the eighty quid IOU

I pushed at him through the slot. He looked at it for a long time.

Then he shook his head, folded it up and pushed it back through the slot.

'Just one hour,' I pleaded.

In the distance the machine-gun started up and I saw the sergeant flinch.

I was going to explain there wasn't any other choice. That I wasn't letting a stranger do it. Someone who didn't know how. Someone who didn't care. Someone who'd hurt her.

But then the sergeant unlocked the door, and I didn't need to say a word.

They were taking Daisy when I got to the line.

Trying to.

Two infantry blokes had ropes round her and were hanging on wide-eyed. They'd have had a better chance trying to rope a sandstorm.

Daisy was magnificent.

Up on her back legs, eyes like liquid fire.

A third bloke was poleaxed on the ground, blood on his head. Next to him, a pair of shears. This mongrel must have been the tail and mane lopper.

I was tempted to kick him in the head myself.

Orders were orders, but bloody hell.

I was also tempted to let Daisy make her point to those that needed to see it. Take her to the officer's mess and let the brass know what she thought of orders like that. Except the brass she needed to kick were oceans away.

A movement over my shoulder.

Another plod, young bloke about seventeen, was aiming a rifle at Daisy, fingers white on the trigger, nearly pooping himself.

I took the gun from him and took the ropes from the other two clowns.

When Daisy saw I was there, she planted her feet back on the ground and slowly calmed down.

'It's all right,' I said to her quietly. 'It's just you and me.'

I saddled her up and we walked to the camp gate. The guard just looked at us. I looked at him. He nodded us through.

I could tell from his face we weren't the first.

We went out into the desert.

Had a long gallop, Daisy's face shining golden in the dawn light, her feet a golden blur.

Then she slowed, circled and chose her spot.

It was time.

I patted her down. Brushed her slowly. Gave her a drink and a feed.

She put her head on my shoulder. I thanked her for being the best mate a bloke could ever hope for. Brushed her some more.

I stopped. I couldn't do it.

There had to be something.

I could dig her a well, here in the sand. The biggest deepest well I'd ever dug. So the water never stopped flowing. So every time I thought of her for the rest of my life at least I'd know she wasn't thirsty . . .

No.

She was looking at me.

Calm. Balanced. She'd thought it through.

I could see in her big gentle eyes she trusted me to do the right thing.

'Thank you,' I whispered to her again.

I put my gun to her head and pulled the trigger.

28

After, as I lay with Daisy, whispering a promise that her daughter would never go to war, never end up a poor tear-streaked body cooling on the sand, a shadow fell over us.

Slowly I lifted my head from Daisy's neck and looked up.

Johnson was sitting on his horse, holding his rifle, staring at me and Daisy.

He didn't say anything.

He didn't have to. I could see from his face why he was here.

He dismounted. Stroked his horse's muzzle.

While he said a quiet and gentle goodbye to her, I hoped she had a son or daughter in a paddock somewhere.

For when Johnson got back home.

Johnson said everything he needed to say, wiped his eyes, then raised his gun.

One shot.

He handed me a spade and we started digging together in the sand.

29

We did our best over there, us blokes.

But it was never in our hands. Not completely. Never is in war.

We were just loyal creatures too, our heads turned this way and that by politicians and generals and the dark waters in our own souls.

That's what we were, all of us.

Just loyal creatures.

A NOTE FROM THE AUTHOR

Loyal Creatures is a story based on history, but it isn't a history book.

However, it is set in a real war, inspired by real events. The desert campaign in Egypt and Palestine was an important part of World War One, and the role the Australian Light Horse played in the fighting was vital.

But Frank and Daisy and most of the other people and animals in *Loyal Creatures* are from my imagination. As you allow them to live and breathe in your imagination, I hope you sense my strong feelings for the many real individuals who inspired them.

The Australian men and women who took part in World War One were all volunteers. Some enlisted well under the official army age of eighteen. Some were even younger than Frank.

Many of the troopers in the Australian Light Horse took their horses with them when they sailed off to war.

The special bond between people and animals has been an important part of Australia's history. Which made what happened to those horses at the end of World War One even more tragic and poignant.

While *Loyal Creatures* isn't a history book, I've tried to ensure that everything in the story could have happened to a young Australian trooper like Frank and to a horse like Daisy.

My own journey with *Loyal Creatures* started in 2012. The National Theatre in London was preparing to bring its magnificent production *War Horse* to Australia. They were also planning a series of workshops around the country, linked to the play and exploring aspects of theatre craft. As a part of this, they wanted a short performance piece about Australian horses in World War One.

My friend Michael Morpurgo, author of the book *War Horse* on which the stage version is based, suggested I write the workshop script. I did, and as I learned more about the experiences of the Australian Light Horse in Egypt and Palestine, particularly in 1918, I knew I wanted to take this story beyond the limits of a twenty-minute monologue. This book is the result.

It wouldn't exist without Michael Morpurgo's wonderful and now legendary story *War Horse*. Thank you, Michael, for allowing my imagination to canter alongside yours for a while. Thanks also to everybody in National Theatre Learning for their encouragement, to Stephanie Hutchinson who produced the workshops, and to Paul-William Mawhinnie and Tim Potter who performed the monologue so brilliantly.

Many other people have helped Frank and Daisy along the way. My heartfelt thanks to Laura Harris, Heather Curdie, Tony Palmer, Alexandra Antscherl, Belinda Chayko, Alex Mann, Richard Atkin, and to David 'Buffalo' O'Brien, who introduced me to a real waler and explained to me how difficult it is to fire a rifle while galloping on a horse.

I hope this story will make you want to find out more about the Australian Light Horse. There are many wonderful real-life stories of real troopers and real horses waiting for you, lots of them to be found in books by real historians.

As well, the Australian War Memorial in Canberra has a vast and magnificent archive of information about the Light Horse and the people and animals who made it a legend, much of it available online.

If you'd like to see a younger version of *Loyal Creatures*, when it was just a frisky colt kicking at the paddock fence, the script of the workshop performance piece is available on the Puffin website (puffin.com.au).

I'm grateful to you for reading this book, and in particular for contemplating the inscription quoted at the beginning.

I like to think that, in our imaginations at least, they've come home.

Morris Gleitzman
April 2014

ABOUT THE AUTHOR

Morris Gleitzman grew up in England and moved to Australia when he was sixteen. After university, he worked for ten years as a screenwriter. Then he had a wonderful experience. He wrote a novel for young people. Now, after thirty-five books, he's one of Australia's most popular children's authors. His books are published in more than twenty countries.

Visit Morris at his website:
www.morrisgleitzman.com

Bumface

His mum calls him Mr Dependable,
but Angus can barely cope. Another baby would
be a disaster. So Angus comes up with a bold and
brave plan to stop her getting pregnant.
That's when he meets Rindi.
And Angus thought *he* had problems . . .

Two Weeks with the Queen

'I need to see the Queen about my sick brother.'

Colin Mudford is on a quest. His brother is very ill and
the doctors in Australia don't seem to be able to cure
him. Colin reckons it's up to him to find the best doctor
in the world. And how better to do this than by asking
the Queen for help?

'A moving and page-turning book' – Sunday Times

Boy Overboard

Jamal and Bibi have a dream. To lead Australia
to soccer glory in the next World Cup.
But first they must face landmines,
pirates, storms and assassins.
Can Jamal and his family survive their
incredible journey and get to Australia?

MORRIS GLEITZMAN

Everybody
deserves
to have
something good in their life.

At least

Once.

Once

Once I escaped from an orphanage
to find Mum and Dad.
Once I saved a girl called Zelda from a burning house.
Once I made a Nazi with a toothache laugh.
My name is Felix.
This is my story.

A little hope goes a long way.

Then

I had a plan for me and Zelda.
Pretend to be someone else.
Find new parents.
Be safe forever.
Then the Nazis came.

After

After the Nazis took my parents I was scared.

After they killed my best friend I was angry.

After they ruined my thirteenth birthday I was determined.

To get to the forest.

To join forces with Gabriek and Yuli.

To be a family.

To defeat the Nazis after all.

Now

Once I didn't know about my grandfather Felix's
scary childhood. Then I found out what the Nazis
did to his best friend Zelda. Now I understand
why Felix does the things he does.
At least he's got me.
My name is Zelda too.
This is our story.